# Finding Love
# At
# Compassion
# Ranch

*To Joe –*
*We all need second*
*chances – Enjoy the*
*story!*

## GAYLE M. IRWIN

*Gayle M. Irwin*
*8/9/2020*

# DEDICATION

This story is dedicated to the founders, staff, and volunteers of the Kindness Ranch. Located in eastern Wyoming, this sanctuary for former research animals provides compassionate care to dogs, cats, rabbits, sheep, horses, cows, pigs, and other animals that have only known pain and loneliness. After becoming socialized and loved on by the Kindness Ranch staff, many of these creatures are adopted by people around the United States. Others live out their years at the sanctuary, experiencing freedom and kindness.

Learn more about the mission and the animals that are cared for at the Kindness Ranch, and those available for adoption, at the organization's website: https://www.kindnessranch.org/

Although the setting for this book is based on a real non-profit organization that helps former research animals, this is a work of fiction. Similarities to real people or events are entirely coincidental.

# ACKNOWLEDGMENTS

I want to thank all my writer friends in both of my Casper writers groups who encourage, empower, and enlighten and challenge me. I also want to thank my beta readers and proof readers, including Jan Anderson, Marian Kingdon, and Judy Lund; and I want to thank and acknowledge my parents, Earl and Marcia Mansfield, who nurtured my love for nature and for animals, and who ensured we took a family vacation to Yellowstone National Park every few years – because of those experiences, that region of the U.S. not only touched my soul, but also provided a home for a time, and, decades later, that area remains special to me. I also want to acknowledge the many animal rescue organizations who do the hard work of taking care of homeless, abandoned, unwanted, fearful, and abused/used animals, providing love, compassion, and sanctuary, oftentimes helping those creatures heal from trauma and find new, caring people and homes: I salute, admire, and thank you!

# Prologue

***EIGHTEEN MONTHS.*** *It's been eighteen months since Daniel died.* Those thoughts ricocheted through Erin Christiansen's brain as she stared upon the majestic Yellowstone Lake. Cabin #15 had been her refuge at the lodging facility within the national park for two nights. One more to go before she again embarked on her journey—returning to the large house in Florida, devoid of her husband's presence for the second summer.

Morning light kissed the still snow-capped mountains to the south. Fuchsia, bluebonnet, and apricot hues danced in the dawn sky. Mornings were Daniel's favorite time of day. They had shared many dawns during their twenty-six-year marriage, including numerous ones along Florida's beaches. *Daniel would have enjoyed watching this sunrise.* Erin's heart contracted as a longing to share the Yellowstone National Park sky with him enveloped her.

A small paw grazed her leg and interrupted her thoughts. Erin leaned down and scooped up her recently-adopted Cavalier King Charles spaniel. She cradled the small dog in her arms.

"I'm so glad you'll be with me, Winston," she whispered into her furry friend's ear. "Last year was hard; now, I now have you for company. I hope you'll like your new home."

For the hundredth time since Erin claimed Winston for her own, she swore the little canine smiled at her before licking her cheek.

# Chapter 1

A COBALT sky gleamed above Wyoming's western meadows and mountains the next afternoon. The late July sun blazed through the windshield of Erin's Toyota Corolla hybrid. She maneuvered the car down a gravel road toward the ranch buildings she had seen from the highway. Having visited this place only once, she relied on her new vehicle's GPS to guide her to the proper turnoff from the highway. The sedan ambled along, stirring up dust. She perceived the area lacked water from the tan grasses along the fence line and the brown shrubbery in the distance. Erin remembered her sister's parting advice from four days ago: "That region can be dry this time of year, so be careful with any potential sparks from your car and be sure to carry plenty of water." Erin heeded Rhiann's words, carrying three one-gallon jugs of the liquid in her car. She was less familiar with western states, and she respected her sister's six years of southwestern Montana residency.

More than a month ago while staying with Rhiann, Erin had pledged two weeks of volunteer service at Wyoming's Compassion Ranch. That promise brought her to this gravel drive. After spending more than five months with her sister and brother-in-law for the second year in a row, Erin planned to reunite with her son and daughter at the family's Florida home before her young adult children returned to college for the fall semester.

Erin stopped the car in front of a large, red barn. She sighed as she glanced around. "I can do this," she said aloud.

A whimper from the passenger's seat caused her to glance at her occupant. She reached her hand and scratched the top of her dog's head. "We can do this together, can't we, Winston?"

The small spaniel thumped his curly tail in affirmation.

Again, she gazed at the building before her and recalled horses sheltered in stalls inside. When she and Rhiann visited two months ago, the animal sanctuary had received four Belgian draft horses that had been injected with cancer drugs. The Oklahoma research facility kept the mares for ten years, conducting more tests and observing outcomes. Compassion Ranch received them after the drug trials. The non-profit's mission of providing sanctuary for former research animals offered the horses, and other creatures, a home for the rest of their lives. Upon learning more about Compassion Ranch and meeting some of the temporary and long-term four-legged residents during that visit two months ago, Erin knew she didn't want to leave the area without helping in some way. Volunteering during her drive back to Florida offered her that opportunity.

Erin stepped out of the Corolla. After closing the driver's side door, she lengthened her body against the side of the red car. Kinks in her lean legs and toned arms loosened as she stretched. The three-hour drive from Lake Yellowstone to Compassion Ranch along narrow, winding, and mountainous roads left the Florida woman weary in body and spirit. Erin twisted first left and then right. The cotton green capris and loose-fitting linen blouse she wore moved easily. Erin stood on tip toes and reached skyward. After a few more stretches, she walked toward the sprawling house near the barn. She remembered this dwelling served as the organization's office. She hoped Maggie, the director, would be inside since she had arrived an hour earlier than scheduled.

As she reached the porch, Erin heard hoofbeats on the road. She turned and waited for the animal and its rider. The man, dressed in a brown cowboy hat, leather chaps covering jeans, and a short-sleeved blue shirt loped the buckskin horse toward the building. When he reined the animal closer to Erin, she noticed the dark leather work gloves upon the man's hands. She also took quick note of brown hair tinged with gray protruding from under his coffee-colored Stetson. His tanned, chiseled face sported a goatee, and a large smile graced his face. The man tipped his hat like a cowboy in a western movie.

"Good afternoon. May I help you, ma'am?" he asked in a warm, polite tone.

"I'm here to meet Maggie Henshaw, the director. I'm spending a few weeks volunteering," she replied.

"Oh, so you're the newbie," he said with a grin, pushing his hat back a bit. "Maggie told me to expect you. She's at a Chamber of Commerce meeting in town. I can take you to your cabin so you can get settled in. Maggie said she'd meet up with you when she returns."

"That would be wonderful. I'd appreciate your help."

Erin noticed the man studying her.

"Your voice sounds vaguely familiar. Have we met before?" he asked.

Erin shook her head. "I don't think so. I'm not from around here."

"Neither am I. There's just something about you... Where are you from?"

"I live in Florida now and have for many years. My husband was in the Air Force, so we moved around a lot, especially in the early years."

"Hmm," the cowboy mused. He shrugged his

broad shoulders and dismounted from the horse. "Never been to Florida."

He walked to Erin and extended his hand. "Happy to have you aboard. Maggie has you set up in one of the volunteer cabins. Sorry, I didn't catch your name."

Erin smiled. "That's because I didn't give it yet. I'm Erin Christiansen."

The man stared at her. "There was an Erin in my high school. Erin Kelly."

Her eyes grew wide. "That's my maiden name."

The man broke into another grin. "Well, I'll be! It is you! I'm Michael Jacobs, Mike Jacobs."

Erin gazed at him in surprise. "Mike! Well, this is amazing! I remember you planned to attend veterinary school and set up a clinic near Seattle."

He nodded. "I did all that. I sold my practice four years ago and came out here, first just to volunteer for a time. Now I'm the ranch manager." His voice sobered. "Maggie told me you lost your husband a few years ago—I'm very sorry, Erin."

She gave him a wobbly smile. "Thank you. It's been about eighteen months, but some days … well, there are days when it's still very difficult."

Mike nodded. "I understand." She looked at

him. "I lost my wife five years ago."

Compassion flooded Erin's face. "Oh, Mike! I'm sorry!"

He gave her a lop-sided, sad smile. "Thanks. Her death was the main reason I sold the practice. The boys had entered college, and I needed a change."

"So, you came to Wyoming to work here?"

He grinned. "Wasn't my intention, but after spending a few days volunteering, I was hooked!"

She heard the enthusiasm in his voice. As he continued smiling, Mike added, "Well, Erin, I must say, you're just as lovely as you were in high school."

Instantly, Erin's brain leaped back thirty-three years to a moonlit spring night. Mike escorted her from his car to the front of her grandparents' light blue farmhouse. Her silken indigo skirt swished across the concrete steps as she carefully climbed the three stairs to the porch. Under the night sky, Mike's lips brushed hers with tenderness. Her first kiss.

Erin pressed her lips together at the memory and looked into his hazel eyes. She gave him a slight smile.

"I don't know about that but thank you for the compliment."

He tipped his hat again. "Well, I think you are. Of course, I always thought of you as beautiful."

Surprise appeared on her face. "You did?"

His smile faltered a bit. "I was too shy to tell you. I tried to drop hints..." He shrugged and then smiled again. "I would never have guessed I'd see you here. I'm glad, though. I thought about you over the years. We have a lot of catching up to do."

# Chapter 2

**AFTER TYING** his horse to a post in the barn, Mike drove his green pickup, leading Erin to her temporary living quarters. He gripped the steering wheel, and his heart thundered in his chest. The pounding began when he recognized his high school sweetheart, even though he attempted to be nonchalant. Of course, she didn't know he'd considered her a love interest in those days because he had been reluctant to tell her. When Mike confided his feelings to his then-best friend, Derek had reminded him of his aspirations to become a veterinarian.

"What good will it do to tell her? She's going to Boise for college, you're headed for Seattle — long distance romances, especially for someone career-focused like you, don't work. You'll break her heart," Derek had said.

A discussion later with Mike's father confirmed Derek's advice. Therefore, he kept his feelings secret from Erin. Yet, he never forgot the dark-haired girl with auburn highlights who joined his senior class after the death of her parents. The closest he came was when his lips claimed hers on the porch of her grandparents' home after senior prom.

Now, as Mike turned his truck to the left and parked near a round, wooden building, he dismissed the images and conversations of the past and willed his heart to slow.

Three guest lodges stood in a semi-circle, timbered woodlands separating the cabins. Surrounded by lodgepole and Ponderosa pines and several quaking aspens, the yurt-style buildings featured three large windows, two medium-sized glass panels, and a small pane on the right side of each structure. A railed, wooden porch encircled half of the cabins.

He jumped from the driver's side of his pickup and waited a few minutes as Erin parked her Toyota sedan. Mike watched her rummage around the front seats. As he walked to the porch, he inhaled a deep breath and then exhaled. By the time Erin stood in front of him, he managed to quell his heart and give her a sincere smile.

"Welcome to your new abode for the next few weeks."

Erin glanced around. "Such a peaceful setting."

"Yes. Doctor McKenna, who started the sanctuary, knew the staff and volunteers would need lodging, so he chose this location for the housing because of the tranquility," Mike responded. "These are guest and volunteer quarters and below, to the northeast of the barn, are the staff cabins."

Erin craned her neck as Mike pointed to four cabins in the distance below.

"Mine is the last one on the far side. Caring for former research animals can be stressful, trying to socialize them and calm their fears. Knowing what many of these creatures have endured can be heart-wrenching, so coming to a place like this, like the cabin I have, helps staff and volunteers unwind and relax."

Mike turns and his lanky legs claimed the three steps to the porch in two strides. He pulled out a set of keys from the side pocket of his jeans and unlocked the front door of Cabin #3. He opened it wide enough to allow Erin, who had joined him on the porch, to pass. Her nearness as she walked by caused his heart to skip. He sucked in a breath and pasted on a smile when she looked at him. She continued into the foyer, and he followed. Erin surveyed the inside of the cabin.

"Very lovely," she murmured.

He thought the same, but not about the cabin. He realized the woman standing inside this space was as enchanting as the 17-year-old girl he'd met decades before.

"Yes, lovely indeed," he whispered.

ERIN CLENCHED and released her hands, fighting to still the quivering of her body. Her response to Mike's nearness caught her off-guard. The spell broke when he asked, "You okay, Erin?"

She glanced at him then at her rigid arms. She again flexed her fingers.

"Gripping the steering wheel, I guess. I've been driving for several days and coming over that huge pass from Yellowstone—well, I'm not used to such roads. I'm just a bit pent up, that's all." She smiled and then breathed in and out. "I just need a walk and some time to relax."

"Well, as you probably noticed, Compassion Ranch offers both opportunities."

The warmth and width of his smile caused Erin's heart to flutter again. She looked away from him as she stepped into the nearby galley kitchen.

"This looks cozy and functional," she said.

"All of the guest cabins have everything a person needs for an enjoyable stay," Mike affirmed. "All you need is your food."

"I assume Cody has grocery and other stores, not just tourist shops."

He nodded. "No mall, but a decent downtown plus two grocery stores off the main street. Restaurants, too, if you're inclined to go out now and then."

"I have enough food for a few more days. I can plan a trip into town later."

"It's a fun community, especially in the summer. Concerts, rodeos, art shows…plus the famous Buffalo Bill Historical Center."

"That's certainly something I want to see! Rhiann told me about it, and of course I saw it from the outside when we drove through a few months ago."

Mike's eyebrows raised. "You were here before?"

Erin nodded. "Rhiann brought me to Yellowstone in early June. We stayed a few nights in Gardiner and travelled around a bit. One of those side trips was to Cody and a stop here. That's when I decided to come back to volunteer before heading home."

"My sons were visiting then – we were likely on one of our fishing trips."

"How many kids do you have?"

Mike smiled. "The two boys. Both college students."

"I have a daughter and a son, also college students."

"We have a lot of catching up to do."

Erin smiled and nodded. "I'll be here two weeks. Speaking of, since I start tomorrow, I'd best get my things and settle in."

"I'll help you unload," Mike said.

"No need. I don't have much. Besides, I should get Winston out for a walk. He hasn't had a break since we left the east gate of Yellowstone."

"Winston?"

Erin smiled and nodded. "My dog. He came into my sister's rescue three months ago, and I just fell in love."

"Rhiann has a rescue? I'd like to hear more about it sometime."

Again, Erin nodded. "I'll be happy to tell you. Thanks for bringing me to the cabin, Mike. I look forward to starting my volunteer duties tomorrow. I understand I report to Leslie, the head caregiver for dogs and cats."

"Yes. You'll meet her at the Kitty Castle. We passed it on the way up here."

"First though I need to get together with Maggie to complete some paperwork."

"As I said, she'll come see you when she gets back from the meeting. Maybe you can finish that up then."

Erin shrugged. "We'll see. After I walk Winston, I want to unpack and relax."

"Anything you need, just let me know," Mike said. She looked at him and arched her eyebrows. He shrugged. "As ranch manager, one of my jobs is to make sure our guests are comfortable and have what they need."

"Oh, of course," Erin said, a slight blush crawling up her neck. "Well, thank you. Thanks for all your help."

"My pleasure," Mike said, his smile again widening across his face. Then, he shook his head. "I still can't believe ... after all these years ..."

She smiled back. "Yes. Such a coincidence!"

Their eyes caught and held a moment.

"Well, again, welcome," Mike said. "I don't know if Maggie told you or not, but twelve beagles arrive in three days and ten cats by the end of the week. We're expecting two people from Colorado in a few days to volunteer, so the three of you will be of great help once we get the additional animals. Who knows – you may find another furry friend to adopt as a playmate for Winston!"

"My daughter wants a cat, maybe two, now that she's in her last semester of college. So, an adoption is certainly possible, but cats, not dogs." She grinned. "Winston's a pretty spoiled boy."

Mike grinned in return. "I've had one of those."

He held the door open for her as he stood on the porch. Erin didn't look at him as she walked past, but she again felt her pulse quicken and her heart pound at his proximity. Understanding how he felt about her when they were seniors in high school caused her palms to sweat as she brushed by him. *How can this happen when Daniel died less than two years ago?* Erin willed her heart to return to normal as she walked to her car, Mike following.

Erin opened the Corolla's passenger door. Winston, leash clipped to his collar, jumped from the vehicle. Mike chuckled and crouched to the ground. Holding a fist out for the dog to sniff, he commented, "What a cute little guy!"

"I think so," Erin responded. "His owner went into a nursing home and couldn't have him anymore. Her family members were too busy to take care of him, so when the town vet in Rhiann's area contacted her about re-homing him, she didn't have to look far. He's a delightful companion!"

Mike nodded. "I can imagine. I used to have

to do that for clients, too—find new homes for their animals. Sad situations sometimes." He scratched Winston's feathery ears. "Welcome to Compassion Ranch, Winston." He rose and looked into Erin's eyes. "You too, Erin."

She smiled. "Thank you, Mike. I'm looking forward to my stay and to helping out."

"Well, I'll let you and Winston get on with exploring and settling in." He reached into his pickup and pulled out a business card from a stack in a cubicle on the driver's side. "Here's how to reach me on my cell phone. I'm often in the large pasture these days as some of the fencing needs repair. If I'm not there, I'm likely at the barn taking care of the livestock. Give me a call if something comes up or you need anything."

She nodded. "Speaking of stock—how are those Belgian horses that came in during the spring? The ones that were part of cancer research."

He grinned. "You heard about those, uh? Well, they're all doing rather good right now. They have free range of two pastures. If you want to see them sometime, I'd be happy to take you out there."

She smiled and nodded. "I'm not the best horsewoman, but yes, I'd like to see them."

"We'll plan a date...err, I mean a day to go do that."

Keeping the smile on her face, Erin nodded again. "Great! Well, I'll see you later, Mike."

He tipped his hat at her. "Have a good rest of your day." He smiled as he looked down at her dog. "You, too, Winston!"

He climbed into his pickup and started the engine. With another smile at Erin, Mike backed the truck onto the graveled lot. After a glance and a wave, he drove from the cabin toward the barn. After a moment of watching his pickup, Erin tightened Winston's leash around her hand.

"Well, little one, let's walk the kinks out of our legs and then go get settled into our cabin."

Winston looked at her and gave a yip and a wag of his tail.

# Chapter 3

**ERIN SAT** in an Adirondack chair on the cabin porch that evening. A glass of iced tea in her hand, she surveyed the pine-laden forest encompassing the wooden structure. Sunset sprinkled apricot, peach, and tangerine across the sky, creating sparkles of varied light upon the needles and leaves of the nearby trees. Shadows danced among the surrounding rocks and low-growing junipers on the forest floor. A slight breeze ruffled the tree branches, like a hen tousling her feathers. The tranquil evening quieted Erin's unsettled heart and mind.

The encounter with Mike, his confession of how he'd felt as a teenager, and her own response not only to the news but to his presence, rattled her. *I'm a widow—why am I feeling like this?* Erin shook her head. *It must just be the response to knowing how he felt back then.* She smiled. *It is flattering. Neither of us are the same, though; too much time has passed.*

She also experienced a pang of loneliness. After several months with her sister and her sister's husband nurturing additional healing after Daniel's death, Erin discovered she missed their companionship. She looked forward to seeing her children—young adults now—but she also knew she needed time alone. Her heart needed more healing, more adjusting, and this peaceful place offered that quiet balm.

*Peace. That's what this place represents for both animals and people,* Erin thought, again soaking in the sights and silence surrounding her. Compassion Ranch gave peace to the animals taken in after medical, pharmaceutical, and agricultural research, providing that for which the sanctuary was christened: compassion. No more poking and prodding, no more pain and loneliness for the dogs, cats, horses, cows, rabbits, and other animals used in research. Peace and compassion – just what Erin also needed.

Losing her retired Air Force husband to cancer had rocked Erin's steady world. She always worried when he deployed but had never considered his retirement would end so abruptly with a brain cancer diagnosis. The strong man she'd always known shriveled before her eyes... and then he died. The months spent in Montana assisting Rhiann and Levi at their animal sanctuary during the past two years helped her grieve with loved ones. Her adult children had spent their spring break this year at the ranch, too, continuing to mourn their father and helping their mother through her own sorrow. Erin remained until last week, aiding Levi and Rhiann with the rescued animals as well as researching and writing grants. Now the return to the home she once shared with Daniel awaited her.

However, this time she wouldn't be alone. Erin reached down and scratched the top of Winston's head as he lay on a blanket next to her chair. His soft crown eased her sorrow and loneliness. She was thankful he was with her and that he'd be with her in the Florida house. She welcomed this time for herself and the opportunity to immerse herself in helping others. That's how she traversed the grieving process. She had done the same when she and Rhiann lost first their parents as teenagers, and many years later, the grandparents who finished raising them.

This new chapter of her life unfolded – that of a widow – but perhaps more than just that label awaited as well. The only way to find out was to turn the page by stepping into the life that lay ahead.

A woman's voice and two taps on the side of the cabin interrupted Erin's thoughts.

"Knock, knock."

Erin looked to her right. Maggie, the director of the sanctuary, stood on a step leading to the porch. Erin started to rise from her chair.

"No, don't get up," Maggie said, navigating the stairs. "You look comfortable." She walked to Erin and extended her hand. "Good to see you again, Erin."

"You, too, Maggie. I'm happy to be here. I have more tea in the cabin. May I get you a glass?"

The director shook her head and sat on the Adirondack chair next to Erin. "No, thank you. I can't stay long." She looked at Erin. "We are certainly happy to have you here! Did Mike fill you in on the animals we're expecting?"

Erin nodded. "He did. I'm looking forward to helping."

"We need it! We don't have as many volunteers this time of year due to schools starting, but between you and the other couple we're expecting, we should have enough hands to help me and the staff as the animals come in."

"I look forward to learning what to do."

"So, you've settled in?"

Erin nodded. "Pretty much. After I take Winston for an evening walk, I'll finish unpacking. After spending a few days in Yellowstone and the drive over from there, I wanted to relax a bit."

Maggie reached her hand down toward the Cavalier, who raised his head for a scratch. "How you doin' there, Winston? Good to see you again. Did you enjoy your second trek through Yellowstone?"

The dog responded with a whine and thump of his tail.

"He's so curious about those bison!" Erin said.

"Most dogs are. I hope you have pictures of him gazing out the window."

"Oh, I do. I texted them to Rhiann and my kids."

"How is your sister?" Maggie asked.

"She's good; so is Levi. The horses began to foal last month, adding to their stock. Levi is excited to have his second crop of colts and foals this year. I think their horse ranch, as well as the rescue sanctuary, is blossoming to become all they've dreamed of."

Maggie nodded. "That's great to hear. Too bad there continues to be a need for rescues and sanctuaries, but I'm glad Rhiann is there for those times of need."

"My daughter, Brittany, plans to go out again next summer for a few months to get more experience. Even though her major is marine biology, she knows she has a job with her aunt and uncle for as long as she wants."

"She's welcome here, too. Although we can't pay her."

Erin nodded. "She knows that. I guess I'm the one testing the waters, so to speak. She may be willing to put in some volunteer time."

Maggie smiled. "If mom's experience is a good one?"

Erin smiled but didn't respond. Maggie's smile faded and she looked directly into Erin's eyes. In a soft voice, she asked, "So, how are your kids doing? How are YOU doing?"

Erin took a deep breath and didn't respond for a moment. "Better. We're all better. But there are days, at least for me, when the whole situation crashes on me like ocean waves. He's been gone about eighteen months, but sometimes it's like I lost him just yesterday."

Maggie patted Erin's hand that rested on the arm of the wooden chair. "Grieving is a process. No one person experiences it the same as another."

Erin nodded. "So, I've been told." She took a deep breath and gave a wobbly smile to Maggie. "I appreciate being here. The peacefulness is exactly what I need as I head back home." Another moment of silence passed, and then she continued, "You say you lack volunteers because kids are back in school, but the visitor numbers in the park don't reflect that. Rhiann says early to mid-July is the worst, but I tell you, I couldn't believe how many people were in the park the past few days!"

Maggie smiled. "Yellowstone is always busy from June to October now. I don't complain though — we receive a lot of visitors here because of the park... and the town of Cody, too. That's how the couple coming in found us."

"What are my instructions for tomorrow?" Erin inquired.

"Come to the office first, around eight, and we'll finish the paperwork. We'll start you with the Kitty Castle in the morning and if you want, you can help at the Dog Palace during the afternoon. Or you can help with dogs the day after."

"Let's hit the ground running! I'll help with both tomorrow."

Maggie nodded. As she rose from her chair, she said, "Sounds good. I'll see you in the morning." She reached down and patted Winston's head. "Nice to see you again, Winston. I hope you and your mom enjoy your stay with us at Compassion Ranch."

"Maggie," Erin said. The fifty-five-year-old black-haired woman stopped and looked at her. "Did Mike say anything to you about me being here?"

"Just that you had arrived, and he helped you get to your cabin. Why? What else might he have said?"

"Turns out we know each other." Maggie's eyebrows raised. "We attended the same high school when I was a senior."

"Well, that's interesting!"

Erin smiled. "Isn't it though? Of all things,

he recognized my voice."

"Really? You must have made a big impression on him in high school." A blush came to Erin's face. She said nothing in response. "You know his wife died about five years ago?"

Erin nodded her head. "He told me. He and I lost touch after graduation. I often wondered about him. He was very kind to me as the new kid in school."

Maggie nodded. "That's still Mike, a kind, compassionate guy. Besides being our ranch manager, he also gives us his veterinary skills. Saves us a lot of money. He's a hard worker and a caring man. We're lucky to have him at the sanctuary."

"I remember he wanted to become a veterinarian, and he planned to attend the University of Washington in Seattle. Something more might have come from our friendship, but he went to Seattle and I went to Boise." Erin smiled as she recalled her senior year. "He took me to spring prom and the after-graduation party."

Maggie looked at her. "Sounds like lovely memories." When Erin didn't respond, she continued, "His wife died in a car accident—slick roads and someone ran into her."

Erin shook her head. "So sad. It's hard to lose a spouse, no matter how that loss comes about."

A moment of silence passed between the two women.

"A few years after her death, when both of his boys were in college, Mike left the big city to do some traveling," Maggie said. "He learned about us while in the area and, like you, came to visit and volunteer. We had an opening for a ranch manager, and he stayed. I'm grateful he did—he's a true asset to Compassion Ranch."

"I'm glad he's found a new calling," Erin responded. "Perhaps I will as well."

She stood and extended her hand. "Well, I'd better take Winston for another walk before dinner. I'll see you in the morning."

Maggie also stood and then shook hands with Erin. "Enjoy your stroll and sleep well."

"Thank you. I'm sure I will."

Erin watched Maggie walk down the steps and to the driveway. The director strolled down the road toward the office. Erin turned to her dog, now standing, and said, "Well, Winston. Time to wrap up our evening. What do you say — a walk and then a treat?"

The little dog stood and gave her his spaniel grin.

MIKE SAT on an upholstered aspen log chair on the porch of his cabin. He basked in the evening sunset, relishing his favorite time of day. The crimson and tangerine sky, the songbirds giving their last trills of the day, the settling of the livestock at the barn and in the pastures—each sight and sound brought a smile to his face and comfort to his heart.

However, this night, the middle-aged veterinarian, still dressed in his work jeans and brown cowboy boots, experienced a different sense. An unsettling. A clamp upon his heart. He'd never forgotten Erin, but he'd been able to bury his feelings. Until today.

Could her appearance at Compassion Ranch mean a fresh start? Each had married another, but now here they were, hundreds of miles from where they first met. Did her arrival indicate a new chapter in each of their lives? Or was it simply coincidence?

He wondered what Erin's life had been like since high school. *Did she become a nurse like she planned? What are her children like? How are they all handling Erin's husband's passing? Perhaps now is not the time to resurrect thoughts and feelings from more than thirty years ago—she needs time and space to heal. Then again, I know what it's like to experience the loss of a spouse; I can help her travel that road.*

These thoughts raced through his mind and heart as the sun dropped below the horizon.

# Chapter 4

**SHADES OF** apricot, peach, and orange graced the western Wyoming sky as sunrise cascaded from mountains to valley floor. Mike stood inside Compassion Ranch's large red barn. He removed Cisco's bridle from a peg on a sturdy wall, removed a curry comb from another hook, and walked to the buckskin's stall. As he stroked Cisco's back and flank, he spoke in a quiet tone.

"I hope you slept well, my friend. We have a lot of hills to climb today. There's a few more horses joining us in about ten days—I need to make sure all pastures are secure because we're going to need to move a few of your friends to make room for the new ones."

The buckskin snorted a response, bringing a smile to Mike's face. He patted the horse's side and said, "Finish up your breakfast while I feed the rest of the stock theirs. I'll see you again shortly."

Mike closed the stall's gate and as he walked to the front of the barn, he heard Cisco munching hay from the wooden trough in his stall. Mike grabbed two sections of hay and exited the barn by the already opened large back door. He sprinkled the feed and coaxed five sheep who resided in the small enclosed arena to come eat. They obliged. After he patted a few of the woolly creatures, he glanced up the hillside toward the guest cabins. A few faint lights flickered from the one occupied by Erin. The other three remained dark. Lights on the hill—how many times in the past few years had Mike seen that? Numerous.

Compassion Ranch was becoming more popular as a destination for visitors and many became volunteers. Some even adopted one or more dogs or cats before leaving. However, this morning, the lights from Cabin 3 made him pause. His feelings tangled like vines wrapping around a fence. *She's an early riser,* he noted. *Maybe that's a result of being a military spouse. Or maybe the time change—it's two hours earlier in Florida.*

Mike sighed. *I really don't need to complicate my life ... or hers. I just want to get reacquainted as a friend and learn more about her life these past many years. Do I dare drive up there?*

Mike walked to his pickup, and after settling into the driver's seat, he started the engine.

AS SHE wiped off the kitchen counter, Erin heard a truck engine motoring up the hill near the cabin. She glanced out the window near the sink and saw a dark green Ford F-250 truck park near her Corolla. Erin watched as Mike stepped from the truck. A moment later, she heard his cowboy boots on the porch. She opened the front door and smiled at him.

"Good morning."

He removed his Stetson and answered, "Good morning to you. I hope it's not too early?"

Erin shook her head. I just finished up the dishes and was going to take Winston for a walk. I have coffee on – would you like some?"

He smiled and nodded. "That would be great."

As Erin returned to the small kitchen, Mike walked inside. Winston sauntered to him, the dog's tail wagging earnestly."

"Mornin' to you, too, boy," Mike acknowledged, holding his hand out.

Winston sniffed, and Mike gave the dog a quick pat to his head, Mike took a seat at the table, and Erin set a steaming cup of coffee before him.

"I didn't mean to bother you, but I saw lights on, and I just wanted to make sure everything's okay."

Erin smiled. "Everything is fine. I've been an early bird for many years, and with this part of the country being two hours behind Florida time, it's really easy to wake up and move around."

Mike returned her smile. "I imagine that's true. I take it you like sunrises?"

She nodded. "Daniel loved sunrises, so I grew to enjoy them, too. I wasn't much of an early bird when I was younger."

"Daniel—your husband?"

Erin nodded. "He especially enjoyed sunrises on the beach."

"I imagine they are quite beautiful."

Silence passed between them for a moment.

"Oh, I'm sorry—I forgot to ask if you want sugar or milk?"

Mike shook his head. "No, black is fine."

"Are you sure? I have some."

He smiled. "No, really, I take it black."

Erin sat across from him, a cup of coffee in front of her. "Me, too," she said with a smile. "What are you doing up so early?"

"Pretty much my regular routine," Mike explained. "Oftentimes an hour later, but today I need to be in the two higher pastures, fixing fence. We're scheduled to receive some more horses in about ten days, so I need to make sure all fences are secure since we'll be moving horses around later in the week." He paused as he took a sip of coffee. "So, did you and Winston sleep well your first night at Compassion Ranch?"

Erin nodded. "Very restful and peaceful. The furnishings here are quite comfortable. Winston loves the couch!"

Both glanced at the small dog, now sprawled across the plush brown sofa. Mike chuckled.

"Appears so."

Erin noticed how his mouth twitched when he laughed and that a small dimple appeared above his chin on the left side. She caught his eyes observing her. She took another sip of her coffee.

"If you don't mind me asking, Erin, tell me a bit about your life with your husband and children," Mike said in a soft voice.

She took a deep breath, glanced out the picture window in the living room, and replied,

"We married the year I graduated from college and after his cadet school. We traveled a lot for his Air Force duty assignments. We lived in Germany for a time as well as Italy and in the United States. They stationed us in New Mexico, California,

Colorado, South Carolina, and lastly Florida."

"No F.E. Warren in Cheyenne, I take it?"

Erin shook her head, her dark curls bouncing. "No Cheyenne. We had the opportunity and considered it because we would have been closer to Grams and Rhiann. But, by then they were spending winters in Arizona."

"I hadn't realized that," Mike commented.

Erin smiled. "Well, you weren't living in Spokane anymore, I don't think."

He nodded. "True, but I occasionally returned to see family. My parents remained in Spokane until they died."

"I'm sorry to hear they've passed."

"Dad developed cancer—it took him quickly. I was about thirty-five. Mom died about six years ago from a heart attack."

"I'm sorry, Mike," she repeated. "I remember your parents as fine people."

"Yeah, they were. I think about them a lot." He glanced out the living room window. "They would have enjoyed visiting the sanctuary."

She smiled. "My kids would too, I think. Daniel would have also."

A moment of silence passed as they each sipped from their cups.

"Tell me about him. If you don't mind, that is," Mike said.

Erin sighed. "He was intelligent, kind, loving, patient. He loved serving in the military and flying planes. He spoke three languages and enjoyed seeing new places. And he liked helping others."

"Sounds like a fine man."

Erin nodded. "He was. He worked hard, but when he was home, he was family-focused. He was so proud of Brittany and Brian...so proud! Both take a lot after their dad."

"Which one's older?"

"Our daughter, Brittany. She'll finish college next spring. Both she and Brian took time off school when their father died, so they are a bit behind. But they've done well. What about your kids?"

He stood. "I'll fill you in on my life next time. I just wanted to check in, like I said, since I saw your lights on. Now I gotta get back to the barn and get Cisco ready for our outing."

"Cisco?"

He smiled. "My horse. Let me know when you might have time for a ride to see the Belgians. We've got a few steady horses here I think would suit you."

Erin stood and walked him to the door.

"Thanks for stopping by and checking on me and Winston."

Mike looked directly into her sea-green eyes. "It's good to see you again, Erin. I hope you enjoy your day."

"Thanks, Mike. You, too."

He nodded at her, opened the door, and walked toward the porch steps. She watched him leave. A moment later, she closed the door and leaned against it.

# Chapter 5

**ERIN SAT** in Maggie Henshaw's office, a large room in an older farmhouse with two tall bookshelves and a refurbished walnut desk. The two women chatted politely as Erin completed the final page of the volunteer forms.

"Obviously, your background check came back great," Maggie said. "I'm so happy you decided to spend some time with us on your way back to Florida. As we discussed, your help is needed right now as we prepare for and receive more animals in a few days."

Compassion Ranch's executive director folded her hands upon her desk. Erin glanced at the dark-haired woman and smiled.

"I'm happy to be here," she responded. "There. All done."

Maggie accepted the papers Erin held out. "Thanks. We just needed that last bit about your vehicle in case something happens to it while you're here—like hail damage or an accident."

"I appreciate you waiting until I got here. I

purchased the Corolla while in Montana, so I had a dependable vehicle for the drive back to Florida."

"So, just my curiosity here, but why are you driving? An airline would get you back home faster."

Erin shrugged and smiled. "There's a lot of this country I haven't seen despite my husband's Air Force career. It's late summer and less weather worries than other times of the year. Plus, I figured a new car would last many years, and I'll hand off the vehicle Daniel and I had to Brittany for graduation, giving her a newer vehicle to start her after-college life."

Maggie nodded. "Sounds like all good reasons. So, are you ready to get started?"

Erin's smile grew wider. "I certainly am!"

The two women stood. "Then, let's head over to the Kitty Castle!"

"Oh, and while I'm thinking about it, if you need help with publicity or grant-writing, I'd be happy to do that, even while I'm in Florida," Erin said. "I helped some non-profits back home over the years, something I will get back into, and I assisted Rhiann with some grants. If I can help you in those ways by email and phone, I'd be glad to."

Maggie smiled. "That's great to know. My administrative assistant, Kaitlyn, who you met out front..." Erin nodded. "She takes care of most of that, but if we find ourselves in need of additional help, I'll keep you in mind."

The two women walked out of Maggie's office. Kaitlyn Murray, a twenty-seven-year-old tall, willowy woman, looked up from the copy machine and acknowledged Maggie and Erin with a nod.

"I'm taking Erin to the Kitty Castle to work with Leslie this morning," Maggie told her assistant. "Then, I'll go to the barn and check on Hope. Mike said she was perkier this morning when he fed her."

"That's good news," Kaitlyn replied. "Maybe she'll be able to get out to the pasture sooner than we thought."

"That would be nice. Fresh air and sunshine will do that lamb a lot of good," Maggie responded. "See you in about an hour."

"I'll have that report ready for you to review."

Maggie smiled. "Excellent! Thanks, Kaitlyn."

"See you later. Again, welcome aboard, Erin — we're happy you're here."

Erin smiled at the young woman. "I'm glad to be here."

"Oh, and Kaitlyn," Maggie began, "Erin has experience helping non-profits with publicity and grant-writing. I told her we might call on her sometime if you need an extra set of eyes or pair of hands."

Erin noticed the expression on Kaitlyn's face briefly reflect surprise. The younger woman's voice stammered slightly as she said, "Oh. Well... well, certainly, yes, if we were to need extra help. So far, though, I've been able to handle things. But, uh, thank you—that's kind of you."

"My pleasure," Erin replied with a smile. "See you later."

Kaitlyn nodded. Maggie and Erin stepped out of the main office and walked to Maggie's Chevy pickup. They didn't notice the slight frown that crossed Kaitlyn's face.

AS THE morning sun drew higher in the sky, Mike rode his buckskin horse across the low pasture. A group of six cows grazed nearby. In the distance, he saw Maggie's blue pickup pull up at the Kitty Castle, a large, hexagonal wooden yurt with two turrets on either side of the front entrance. He stopped his horse near the fence line and watched as

Maggie and Erin exited the truck and walked inside the building. Mike noticed the relaxed, yet confident way Erin carried herself. He knew she experienced a lot of loss in her life: her parents, her grandparents, and more recently, her husband. He, too, had experienced numerous losses. Perhaps, like him, Erin had found great purpose in helping others, helping her overcome the significant sorrow that life can throw at a person.

Mike tipped his hat back gazed at the summer sky. He drank in the sunlight, the gentle breeze, and the fragrance of wildflowers and grass. Nearby a meadowlark trilled. He smiled at the sound. A fleeting wisp of bright blue zoomed by. Mike's eyes followed the male bluebird's flight to a nearby box attached to a wooden fence post. The creature placed its head inside a hole in the square house, likely dropping an insect or seed into a nest. The bluebird stayed only a moment and then winged across the landscape.

Mike leaned over the saddle horn and patted his horse's strong neck.

"Another beautiful day, eh, Cisco? Time to let you graze while I work on some fence posts. I'll stay clear of the bluebird box — looks like a family took up residence in that one this year. Nice to see 'em, isn't it?"

The gelding nickered, and Mike smiled. "Time for me to get to work, old boy."

He dismounted like an expert and pulled tools from the saddlebags. After staking Cisco near a large sagebrush, Mike began to check the wire.

A FEW hours later inside the Kitty Castle, Erin emptied a bucket of dirty water into the large bathroom sink. She turned the faucet handle and rinsed out the blue tub as well as the mop she had used to clean the floor. The thirty cats living at the Castle sat or lay in the outdoor, fenced enclosure, soaking up sun rays or gazing upon pasturelands and woods surrounding the building. The three-quarter around catipatio featured hammocks, cat beds, carpeted climbing trees, large branches, and high beams. Several toys were also scattered throughout the enclosure.

As Erin finished tidying up the bathroom, she observed the cats housed at Compassion Ranch. Young ones, older ones, black ones, multi-colored ones; long and short-tailed kitties, and shy as well as extroverted cats comprised the company of felines. She smiled at the joy and relaxation she observed. Yet, Erin's heart also felt heavy. All these cats, with more to come, and this was just one sanctuary in one location. Until she began working with Rhiann at the Martha's Montana Animal Rescue, Erin hadn't fully understood the scope of animal rescue and adoption. *When I get back to Florida, I'm going to volunteer somewhere like this, like Rhiann's place,* she told herself. *There's such great need.*

Erin shook out the mop and, stepping out the bathroom door onto a small veranda, she hung the utensil on a hook as instructed by Leslie, the lead animal caregiver. She was to meet the young woman at the Dog Palace after lunch. Leslie had told her she would open the cat doors leading back inside the Castle after the floors dried, allowing the kitties to come inside during the hot July afternoon. Therefore, Erin was free to get lunch for the next seventy-five minutes.

She walked out the front door, securely locking it behind her. As she passed the happy resident felines, she smiled and said, "Goodbye, kitties. I'll see you tomorrow morning again and perhaps we'll have some play time."

She smiled wider as a few meows acknowledged her voice. *Perhaps I will adopt a couple of these cats for Brittany,* she thought. *I'll have to bring Winston to meet them and help choose.*

She began to walk toward her cabin. She enjoyed strolling around the property. All the places she needed to be that day were in proximity of the cabin, so she opted to not drive. She hoped Winston hadn't become too lonely staying in the cabin for three hours. She'd fix lunch for both of them and then take him on another walk before she met Leslie at the Dog Palace for her afternoon volunteer work.

About half-way to the cabin, she heard a pickup looming behind, so she stepped to her right, out of the way, to let the vehicle pass. Instead, the truck came to a stop. Erin looked over as the passenger's side window came down. A smiling Mike sat behind the wheel.

"Would you like a lift to your cabin?"

Erin smiled back. "Sure, that would be nice. Winston will need a walk before I meet Leslie at the Dog Palace, so I can use those spare minutes."

She opened the passenger's side door and hopped into the seat. After she closed the door and secured her seatbelt, Mike drove toward the cabins on the hill.

"So, how was your morning?" he asked.

She smiled. "Good. Leslie showed me the basics of cleaning the cat areas, and I finished the work myself."

"No playtime though, I take it?"

Erin shook her head. "That's in the afternoon during the summer, I understand."

Mike nodded. "Summer temps here can get pretty warm, even though we have the mountains."

They reached Erin's cabin. As she started to exit the truck, Mike said, "I have extra lunch with me today if you want to share and not have to fix something for yourself."

"Whatcha got?"

He reached for a bag in the back of the dual-cab truck. Pulling it forward, he looked inside. "I have roast beef and cheddar sandwiches, some strawberries, and veggie chips."

"And I have a large salad I made earlier today which I'm happy to share. Plus lemonade"

"Sounds like a great lunch!"

Mike grinned at her and jumped from the truck. "I'll set things up on the porch while you get Winston and the salad from the cabin," he said.

"Sounds good."

The two reached the porch and Erin walked to the door. Taking a key from the side pocket of her jeans, she unlocked the door and opened it. A dancing Winston greeted her.

"Hey, buddy," Erin said as she bent down to ruffle his ears. "Did you miss me?"

Erin walked inside the cabin.

"If you'll hand me his leash, I'll take him for a short trek while you get the salad and such ready,"

Mike offered.

"I take it you don't have plates or bowls with you?" Erin asked.

"No. With sandwiches, I generally just use my fingers," Mike replied.

She removed Winston's leash from a hook near the door and handed it to Mike. He clipped the blue plaid mechanism to Winston's collar and said, "Ready for a short walk, Winston?"

The small dog yipped a "yes" and followed Mike off the porch toward some nearby trees. Erin watched them for a moment and then gathered the large salad bowl from the fridge and placed it on the kitchen counter. She removed two small bowls from the cupboard and divided the greens between them. She sprinkled a bit of shredded cheese on top of the salad and reached for the light ranch dressing in the fridge. She decided to place the topping on only one salad for now. Then, she picked up two forks from the utensil drawer. When she heard Mike and Winston return to the porch, she poked her head out the cabin door and asked, "Is ranch dressing okay?"

"Perfect."

"It's light, low-fat."

"Even better."

Mike smiled at her and then tied Winston's leash to a porch rail. He set up a small side table with the food items from his bag. Erin walked out with the salad bowls and forks. She returned to cabin to pick up two glasses of lemonade she had poured. She and Mike sat on the wooden chairs stationed to the porch and began to eat.

"I believe you were going to tell me about your life," Erin prompted Mike. "Maggie mentioned to me you were traveling when you learned about Compassion Ranch – true?"

Mike looked at her and nodded. "After selling my practice, I decided to visit Wyoming. I spent time in the Jackson Hole area and visited Grand Teton National Park. I spent another week in Yellowstone, sight-seeing, hiking, horseback riding, and taking a few classes at the park's institute."

"Sounds enjoyable," Erin commented.

Mike smiled. "It was. I wanted to do some more hiking and fishing near Cody, and as I drove out of the park and came closer to town, I saw the sanctuary sign. I stopped by but there was no one in the office. I had reserved a few nights' stay in Cody, and when I stopped at the chamber office to learn about fly-fishing guides, there was a brochure about Compassion Ranch. The next day I talked to Maggie and arranged for a tour. I decided to come back after a few days of fishing and hiking to volunteer for a week. I loved everything about this place, stayed another week, and when she told me about the job opening as ranch manager, I applied." He grinned.

"So much for traveling … or retiring."

A few moments of silence passed between them as each began to eat their lunch.

"What about your practice in Seattle?"

Mike shrugged. "Still going well, as far as I know. Not mine anymore, so I don't pry. Neither of my sons live in Seattle anymore either, so I don't go back but may once in a blue moon. I either go see them or they come here to visit." I do a lot of good here. I love the mission, the work, the location, the peacefulness. I help animals in a variety of ways, including still using my veterinary skills. One of my boys may likely move to the area once he finishes his medical degree."

"What are their names?" Erin asked.

"My oldest is Jacob. He's going into his last year of med school; he plans to be a physician's assistant and has been promised a job with a doctor in Cody. Samuel has two more years until he finishes his engineering degree at Washington State University. His desire is to work in the automobile industry. After their mother died, both boys set their sights on helping others who could lose a loved one in a car accident."

Silence passed between them for a few minutes. "That must have been so hard for the boys and for you."

He nodded and remained quiet for a moment. "It was a shock...for all of us."

"I know the feeling," Erin murmured.

He looked at her and took her hand. In a soft voice, he said, "I know you do."

"Your loss was such a shock," Erin said as she returned his gaze. "Daniel died six months after being diagnosed with brain cancer."

Sympathy welled up in Mike. "No matter the 'how,' a loved one's death is never easy to accept. Grief is a tough road to travel."

Tears welled in Erin's eyes. "We've both experienced tragic losses. Sometimes Daniel's death seems like just yesterday, other times, like forever ago. I still think about my parents, maybe more so in the last year than I did for a long time."

Mike nodded and squeezed her hand again. "Elizabeth died five years ago, but at times it's as you say, like yesterday."

Silence passed between them for a moment. "Grief is a tricky thing," Mike continued. "That's one reason it's important for me to spend time with my sons. They were in high school when Elizabeth's accident happened. College helped them both to re-focus, and they are doing well. They come to the ranch each summer to volunteer for a month, and then the three of us travel somewhere in the region for a few weeks before they head back to school."

She nodded. "I can understand why that's important. My kids came with me to Rhiann's place near Bozeman. They took a semester off after Daniel's passing and so are a bit behind. This year, they spent spring break in Montana plus a month earlier this summer. Now they're getting ready to return to college."

Mike patted her hand, and then they both again began eating some of their lunch.

"What are your kids studying?" Mike asked after he'd chewed a few bites of his sandwich.

"Brittany is a senior at the University of South Florida, and Brian is a sophomore at Florida State. Brittany plans to be a marine biologist, and Brian is studying computer science – he would like to work at NASA."

"Great careers for both of them, I'd say."

Erin smiled. "I think so. They're extremely intelligent, like their father."

Mike looked into her eyes. "Don't sell yourself short, Erin. I remember a bright young lady in high school." He thought he detected a blush as she smiled and then dipped her head. "Did you go into nursing as you planned?"

Erin shook her head. "After my freshman year, I went into teaching and received my elementary education degree. While Daniel and I were in Germany and Italy, I taught English part-time. After the kids were born, I became a stay-at-home wife and mother until they were in junior high and high school, and then I taught English online for about four years. With moving so much, I found it much easier to be an Air Force wife and mom, and then when online education grew popular, I could put my desire to help youngsters back into play."

"Makes sense. I bet you're a great teacher."

She smiled again, and they finished their lunch.

# Chapter 6

**THAT AFTERNOON,** Erin lingered in the Dog Palace play yard. Three tri-colored beagles romped through the grass, relishing the sunshine on their backs. Although still green in many places, tinges of tan and brown indicated summer's wane and autumn's dawn. Yet the blue sky and sun rays reflected the heat of the day. After spending much time inside the large, round, wooden building with its many windows and big, covered, fenced deck, this outdoor frolic would be the last for the pups until evening after supper. Therefore, Erin and the Compassion Ranch staff allowed the dogs one more afternoon play date.

Erin watched the beagles run and chase each other. She mused about their previous life—stuck in cages and stuck with needles. Although research was needed in many ways, especially medical and veterinary research, the conditions many animals, including cats and dogs, endure and the pain oftentimes inflicted upon them, made her shudder. Her heart swelled with joy knowing Compassion Ranch was created specifically to help former research animals like these dogs and the cats she had spent time with earlier in the day.

One of the pups trotted forward, a tennis ball in its mouth. The dog sat in front of Erin, black and brown tail wagging. She smiled and reached down. The beagle dropped the ball and looked at her. As Erin picked up the toy, she heard a woman's voice say, "I think Evie likes you."

Erin turned her head and smiled. "She seems very sweet."

"She is. She's come a long way since her days at a research lab."

Erin chucked the ball across the yard. "Good arm!" the woman said.

Erin laughed. "My son played Little League and on his high school baseball team. I learned quickly so I could keep up with him."

She turned and faced the woman. In a more sober tone, she asked, "How many dogs do you generally care for here, Leslie? At one time."

Compassion Ranch's head animal caretaker, Leslie Barnett, looked Erin in the eye. "It varies. We've had as many as forty at one time plus sixty cats. Many times the animals come in large groups, at least ten and as many as thirty at a time."

Erin shook her head as sadness enveloped her. "And to think—if you all weren't here."

"There was a time we weren't. These animals had nowhere to go until this place came to be."

Erin watched as Evie, ball back in her mouth, trotted to her again. The other two beagles played with each other at the back of the yard, wrestling and rolling, barking, and braying.

"And you're expecting more soon, Maggie told me," Erin said.

She once again reached down and took the ball from the small female beagle. She tossed the yellow toy once again, away from the other two playful pups. Evie chased it down.

"Yes," Leslie responded. "In about two days and then some after that."

"How do you want me to help?"

"We'll need to confirm with Maggie, but we'll likely have you cleaning and playing with these guys and the cats as usual. That way the rest of us as staff can take care of the animals coming in. Mike will check them over medically and vaccinate them and we'll confine them in the barn as we evaluate them. Hopefully, within a few days, we'll be able to introduce them to the pack here."

"Same when the cats come in?"

"As far as your responsibilities, yes. But the Kitty Castle is large enough to segregate new cats from the current ones and we'll introduce the new ones a few at a time to the group. The Castle provides plenty of space because cats need it—and we have felines here longer than canines."

"Why is that?" Erin asked.

"People adopt dogs more often than cats, which is sad for us in many ways, but primarily because the dogs need much more time to socialize with humans. Cats are more independent by nature, so they become available for adoption faster."

Erin smiled as Evie again dropped the tennis ball at her feet. "Does this girl ever take a break?"

Leslie laughed. "She does, but not for long. Beagles are hounds, and their job is to find things. They go long distances after rabbits and such, so to her, a ball is like prey – something to chase down and bring back. It's like she's in the field and she's bringing you back what she's found. People often don't understand, or investigate, the needs of dog breeds before they get them. Different dogs have different energy levels and needs for activity. That's how many end up in animal shelters. People need to do their homework before bringing home a dog like an Australian shepherd, a terrier, or a beagle. We spend a lot of time with our potential adopters educating them on the dogs' needs and hang-ups. We want to make sure each adopter is committed to working with, playing with, and caring for these animals, whether dogs, cats, rabbits, or other animals we take in and look to place in homes."

After a few more throws of the ball and Evie bringing the toy back each time, Leslie said to Erin,

"We'd better get these guys back inside. All their activity in this heat can take its toll, even though they don't want to stop."

Erin laughed. "I really don't either." She looked at the sky and then to the forested and prairie areas around the sanctuary. "It's so peaceful and beautiful here."

Leslie smiled as her gaze also wandered to their surroundings. "It certainly is. I'm blessed to work and live here." She looked at the dogs and clapped her hands. "Hey, friends—time to go inside and cool off!"

She and Erin led the way back into the log-sided building, three beagles with wagging tails following them.

THAT EVENING, Erin strolled alongside her Cavalier King Charles spaniel. After a light dinner of chicken salad and an hour of reading, both accomplished on the porch, she decided to wander to the lower pasture where she had earlier seen a small group of sheep and two llamas. Leash in hand, she walked toward the fenced area; Winston ambled beside her. Occasionally, the little dog stopped to sniff the grass and weeds paralleling the gravel road.

"Lots to smell, isn't there, Winston?" Erin asked, watching him whiff the plants.

He looked up at the sound of his name and presented what some call a doggie grin. Erin smiled and reached down to ruffle the top of the little dog's head. They continued their journey and in about ten minutes, they reached the pasture. Winston watched the strange animals. Six white, woolly sheep grazed close together while two llamas, one black and the other white with brown spots, chewed grass nearby. The slender-necked animals raised their heads and gazed back at Erin and Winston. The Cavalier yipped. Erin reached down and picked him up. As she held him, she said, "Shh, Winston. I know they're strange-looking, but you don't need to antagonize them."

The dog yipped again. The black llama made a strange noise, like a chortle.

"Shh!" Erin scolded her dog. "Let's just enjoy watching them."

She stood there, holding Winston in her arms, and watched the llamas and sheep graze. One of the white animals stepped from the group. Erin immediately realized the ewe was pregnant. She smiled. "Ah, a lamb will be born!"

At that moment, the door to a nearby shed opened and closed. Erin looked to her right and saw

Mike placing the padlock on the small barn-like green building. He glanced over, saw her, smiled, and waved. She returned his smile and nodded at him, unable to wave due to the small dog cradled in her arms. Mike walked over.

"You're working late," Erin commented.

He nodded. "Getting ready for the group of dogs that will arrive in a few days. I needed to check on the vaccines, making sure we have enough."

"And do you?"

He nodded again. "For the dogs. I'll need to get more rabies vaccine for the cats that arrive at the end of the week." He looked at the sheep and llamas. "What do you think of this group of livestock?"

"I'm surprised to see llamas. They're former research animals also?"

Mike shook his head. "No. One of the neighboring ranches had them and gave them to us. Llamas are great protectors of sheep and when we started getting sheep last year, he helped us out."

"He didn't need them for his stock?"

"He has other llamas. These two are getting older. Jet, the black one, is fifteen, and Chip, the spotted one, is close to twenty. Mr. Bellingham, the rancher, has younger ones as he needs them on a regular basis. We don't always have sheep, so when we do, these guys have a job in addition to being grass mowers."

"They make a strange sound."

Mike smiled. "Ah, you heard the llama hum."

Erin frowned. "It sounded more like a chortle. A bit spooky, really."

The smile remained on his face. "Technically, it's called a hum, but the sound can range in intensity, depending on the situation. Females hum to young and all llamas seem to hum when food's being brought to them. If what you heard sounded like a chortle, then, they must have fixated on this guy." He stroked Winston's head. "They're not used to smaller dogs like Winston."

"Well, and 'this guy' tried to play toughie." Erin also stroked Winston's face. She then wagged her index finger at him. "No more of that, mister!"

Mike chuckled, and Erin smiled before returning her gaze to the animals in the pasture.

"Looks like one of the sheep is going to have a lamb," she noted.

Mike nodded. "Likely by the end of the week. Which is good. We have a young ewe who needs a friend. So, once the lamb is weaned, we'll put it with our single gal so they can be buddies."

"Why is one by itself?"

"One of her back legs needed to be amputated."

"Oh, my!"

"She's doing pretty well. But she's also blind in one eye, so having a pal will be good for her. We're looking for the day when we have another lamb who can be Hope's companion."

"May I see her?"

Mike looked at Erin. "She's down at the barn. Feel like walking down there?"

Erin smiled. "Of course. That's what Winston and I are doing this evening—walking."

"Right. Then, let's go."

As they began the jaunt to the barn, Erin noticed Mike's broad shoulders and strong arms. With shirt sleeves rolled up to his elbows, even his forearms flexed with muscle. She tore her gaze away from his brawny body. *I can't be thinking these things.* She refocused on the walk and their surroundings.

"Leslie explained a few things you all do to prepare and welcome new animals," Erin said, attempting to distract herself. "Sounds like you have a lot of work to do."

"True, but it's good work, really good work."

She glanced at him then looked forward again. "You really love being here, don't you?"

"Yes, yes, I do. This organization has a wonderful mission, and I'm hoping next year we'll be able to take in even more animals."

She looked at him again, and he returned her gaze. They stopped walking for moment.

"Maggie and Kaitlyn are working on a grant that would help us build two more buildings – one for dogs and another barn," Mike said. "A lot of livestock is involved with agricultural and cancer research, and we have the property to create more pastures, but not another large barn or a small one out in the distant pastures to shelter additional livestock. We need those things. We also need either another dog building or a large addition to the one we have. So, they are creating a grant to hopefully get some funds for the materials and to hire two more guys to help construct the buildings."

"That's great! I told Maggie and Kaitlyn I can help with grants—maybe I can."

Mike smiled. "Yes, maybe you can."

As they continued their walk to the barn, Erin made a mental note to ask the women about that tomorrow.

BEING NEAR Erin and sharing his thoughts and hopes about the sanctuary with her made Mike feel like a young man again. His routine when the boys were young and Elizabeth was alive had become just that: routine. Here, at Compassion Ranch, nothing was routine. Fixing fence one day, doing veterinary care another day, constructing or repairing stalls, feeding and brushing horses, giving tours to visitors…all the variety as well as the stunning surroundings brought him peace and joy. It also kept his mind occupied. Yet, Erin's appearance at the ranch, and his response to her presence, caught him off-guard. His buried feelings from that senior year of high school resurrected. Yet, he was no longer a boy, and so he had to make sure these thoughts and feelings were legitimate and not just remembrances from thirty-two years ago.

"You're quiet." Erin's soft voice broke into his thoughts.

Mike started and then smiled. "Thinking about tomorrow's construction project," he lied.

"Oh."

Did she sound disappointed? Mike nearly

stopped walking to look at her face but decided against doing so.

"Just lots going on," he added.

Erin nodded. "I understand."

They reached the barn. As he extended his hand to open the door, he looked at her and said in a quiet tone, "Hope knows my voice, so let me speak first so she's not startled."

Erin nodded and waited while Mike unlocked and then opened the side door. He let her pass and stilled his racing heart as she brushed by. He followed Erin, still holding Winston's leash, inside. She stopped, tied her dog's tether to a post, and then let Mike lead the way to the lamb. Mike walked toward a large wooden enclosure on the side of the barn. He spoke in a low tone, "Hey, Hope. I'm back. Want to have a small treat before you go to sleep?"

He picked up a small brick of molasses and oats from a nearby bin. He held it in his right hand as he approached the young sheep's enclosure. Mike's heart always melted seeing this seven-month-old white lamb with black spots. She rose from her nest of hay as he approached. Wobbly on three legs at first, the determined animal waited a moment to steady and then approached Mike with a soft bleat. He broke off a piece of the treat and presented it to her, palm flat. With his left hand, he coaxed Erin to stand beside him. He heard her gasp and muse, "Oh! Sweet thing!"

Mike broke off another piece of the oat mixture and placed it into Erin's hand. "Flat out," he whispered as she started to fold her fingers around the treat.

She did as he instructed. Hope reached her nose toward Erin's extended hand. As the lamb nibbled the food, Mike stroked the creature's left side. "How's the girl this evening?" His gentle tone caused the young sheep to shift and place her face in his hand.

"She really trusts you," Erin commented.

"We're buddies," Mike responded with a smile. "Now that she's able to walk, she follows me out of the barn each morning when I feed the cows. She spends time outside, close to the barn while I take care of the other livestock. Then, she rests in here for part of the day and goes back out in the early evening when I come to again feed the rest of the livestock."

"So, you were just here not long ago."

He shrugged and smiled. "I enjoy hanging out with Hope."

"Why 'Hope?'"

"Why not?" He paused a moment. "She had no hope four months ago. The research facility noticed her lameness and discovered she had cancer of the bone. They were going to euthanize her, but someone on the team learned about us and asked if we wanted to take her. We did but we had to remove her leg. She's slowly adjusting as a tri-pod, as most animals do, at least dogs and cats. She's even learning to play with toys, like bouncy balls and rubber toys with treats inside. In addition to physical healing, Hope, and animals like her, need enrichment activities to stay mentally stimulated. That's part of what we do here, too."

Erin appeared to look at him in amazement.

"What?" Mike asked.

"I'm just in awe of all that goes on here. I'm glad you all are here for these animals."

"I am, too," Mike said as he returned his gaze to Hope. He patted her side once again and then the top of her head. "I certainly am too."

He didn't notice Erin take a sneak peek at him.

# Chapter 7

**THE NEXT** evening, Erin stood by the kitchen sink washing dishes. She stared out the window as she ran the washcloth over a plate in her hand. She hadn't seen Mike all day and somewhere deep inside her heart, she felt disappointed. Erin tried to steer her mind in another direction, remembering the joy of playing with the cats and kittens at the Kitty Castle earlier today. A smile came to her face as she recalled the two young yellow tabby toms that rolled and wrestled together and when she sat on the floor near them, sauntered her way. She engaged them in hide-and-seek with a toy mouse attached to a string. Animals that spent months, even years, in research facilities seemed to implement forgiveness and trust easier and quicker than humans, and that fact touched her heart.

"Those cats may be just the ones for Brittany," she mused aloud.

As she finished drying the small set of dishes and began opening cupboards to put them away, a Toyota Rav 4 spit gravel as it passed her cabin and parked at one across the way. Erin watched as a man descended from the driver's side and a woman exited the passenger's side. The woman opened the door behind the front passenger's side and a sheltie jumped to the ground. Erin smiled as she watched the dog prance around, obviously excited to be out of the vehicle. The couple, followed by their pup, walked to the cabin's porch. Another vehicle approached. Erin recognized Mike's truck, and her heart skipped a beat. She shook her head, silently admonishing herself.

Erin felt paws on her right leg. She glanced down and saw Winston as he dug his little feet into her thigh. She picked him up and helped him look out the window.

"Looks like we have neighbors, little guy. Should we get acquainted?"

The Cavalier gave a small yip, again making her smile.

"You know one of the great things about you, my friend? You help me smile and laugh, even when I don't feel like it. Let's go say hi to our new neighbors and Mike."

Erin took the dog's leash from the hook near the door before she walked out of her cabin. She attached the lead to Winston's collar, set him on the floor, and opened the door. As human and pup stepped onto the porch, Erin heard Mike's voice.

"We're glad to have you here again. Maggie said you may be interested in adopting one of our beagles."

"That's one reason we're here, yes," the other man's voice said. "When we learned Compassion Ranch was getting some new dogs, Lauren and I decided this was the time to return as volunteers."

"And potential adopters," the woman, Lauren, chimed in.

Erin watched as Mike unlocked the cabin door for the couple and presented the key to the man. "Enjoy your stay. We expect the dogs to arrive tomorrow around noon. Leslie will welcome your help with cleaning in the morning while she and I and Maggie prepare the barn for the dogs' arrival."

Erin, stepping from her cabin's porch with her dog, walked Winston closer to the new arrivals. "Hello, neighbors!"

The three people on the opposite porch looked her way. With a smile on her face, Erin approached closer.

"Oh, hey there, Erin," Mike said.

She smiled. "Hi, Mike." She climbed the porch steps to the couple's cabin. However, knowing they had a dog, she commanded Winston to sit and stay then returned her gaze and her smile to the couple. "I'm Erin Christensen. I'm staying in Cabin Three." She nodded toward her place of lodging.

Lauren, a woman about thirty, walked toward her with a smile. "Hi, Erin. My name is Lauren

Griffith, and this is my husband, Jordan."

The two women shook hands while Jordan, a tall man in his early thirties, nodded at Erin and said, "Nice to meet you."

"You both as well."

"Jordan and Lauren visited us in the late spring during a trip to Yellowstone," Mike explained. "They live in Colorado and decided to return and help us with the new animals we're expecting."

"We're heading up to Glacier National Park after our time here and a few days in Yellowstone again," Jordan said.

"What a wonderful trip! I was in Glacier with my sister just last month—it's stunning!"

"Where do you live, Erin?" Lauren inquired.

"Florida."

"Wow! That's a long way!"

Erin smiled. "Certainly is. I'm heading back there after my stay here at Compassion Ranch. I spent time earlier with my sister in Montana."

"You're driving?" Lauren's voice indicated surprise. Erin smiled wider.

"Yes. There's a lot of this country I've not

seen, even though my late husband was in the military. The trip affords me opportunity to see places I've wanted to see but haven't been able to yet. I'm looking forward to visiting some national parks and wildlife refuges along the way."

"Late husband?"

Erin nodded at Lauren's question. "Yes. Daniel died about eighteen months ago. Cancer."

She noticed the couple glance at one another. Lauren returned her attention to Erin and whispered, "We're so sorry."

Erin gave her a quick nod. "I appreciate that." In a lighter tone, she added, "This is my four-legged friend, Winston. He's a rescue."

Lauren bent down to scratch the Cavalier's head. "How sweet! Our girl, Molly, has already claimed the couch for the night. She's a rescued sheltie. Did Winston come from Compassion Ranch?"

"No. My sister has a rescue sanctuary about thirty-five miles from Bozeman, Montana. She turned our great-grandparents' homestead into a haven for dogs, cats, and horses in need of new homes. She and her husband also raise and sell paint and palomino horses."

"Really? I didn't know that," Mike said.

Erin nodded and smiled.

"So, you and your sister were raised in Montana?" Jordan asked.

"No. The ranch once belonged to our great-grandparents; our grandmother was raised there, but she left in the 1940s. Before Grams died, she and Rhiann learned the property was available for back taxes, and fortunately, all worked out for them to buy the place and put it back in our family."

"Wow! That's quite a story," Lauren said.

"I'll say," Mike stated.

Erin looked at him and smiled. "We haven't gotten all of our catching up done."

She saw the couple look at one another again. "Turns out, Mike and I knew each other in high school."

"Another great story," Jordan said.

"Yes, but all for another time, at least for me. I have horses and sheep to feed and secure yet this evening," Mike said, starting to walk toward the steps.

"And I imagine you folks want to get settled in," Erin said as she looked from Lauren to Jordan. "I'll look forward to working with you in the morning. Winston and I still have our evening walk to take."

"See you tomorrow," Lauren acknowledged,

walking back to her husband.

Jordan waved at Erin and Mike and then stepped into the cabin. Lauren followed. Mike walked to Erin and smiled at her.

"How was your day?"

"Wonderful!" she responded with a smile. "I had part of the day off, so I went into town, visited the Buffalo Bill Center, and grabbed a few groceries at the store."

"What did you think of the museum?"

"Amazing! You were right—there's so much to see. I wasn't able to take it all in, but I hope to get another chance before I hit the road back to Florida."

Erin thought she noticed Mike's face fall at her words. However, he plastered a quick grin and said, "It's truly worth spending a day. Maybe I can arrange for Maggie to give us time off together and I could take you."

"Are you sure we should both be gone at the same time?"

Mike shrugged. "With Lauren and Jordan here, we may be able to get away. I'll check with Maggie tomorrow."

Together, Mike and Erin navigated the porch steps and walked toward his truck.

"Want to help me at the barn?" he asked. "You could feed and hang out with Hope."

"I'd love that. It's okay to have Winston along? I can leave him in the cabin if you'd rather."

Mike smiled. "No need. I think they did well the other night. Hope might enjoy the extra company. Best keep him clear of the horses, though."

She nodded and picked up her little dog. Mike opened the passenger's side door and Erin climbed into the pickup, still holding Winston. As she brushed by the muscular ranch manager, a slight flush crept up her neck. As Mike closed the pickup's door, Erin placed Winston on the console between the two bucket seats. She grasped the seatbelt and buckled herself in. She picked up Winston and sat him on her lap as Mike jumped into the driver's side. He started the truck, backed it up slightly, and returned to the gravel road leading toward the animal buildings, including the barn.

AS HE drove, Mike chewed his lower lip. He didn't like to be reminded Erin was at Compassion Ranch for only a few weeks. He really wanted to spend more time with her. He'd talk with Maggie tomorrow about giving him that time, starting with a trip to the museum he so thoroughly enjoyed.

He jolted when he heard Erin ask, "You haven't said much about your wife. Do you mind telling me about her?"

Mike smiled. "Not at all. Elizabeth was incredibly supportive of my veterinary career. She was gentle, loving, devoted, kind, lovely, inside and out, and very smart."

"You must have loved her deeply."

"I loved her, yes. Maybe not as deeply as I should have." He took a large breath and exhaled. "That's my one regret. I was caught up in my career and as long as I provided for my family, I thought that would be enough. I didn't realize how much my time away from home, working late nights, weekends on call, all of that, would impact her and the boys. I missed a lot. I realized that after she died." He took another deep breath. "I guess that's why, when my sons come to the ranch, I spend as much time as I can with them. I make sure we're together at Christmas and during their spring breaks as well."

"That's important for me, too, with my kids," Erin said. "We've spent a lot of time with Rhiann and Levi since Daniel died, me especially. I've needed family. Spending several months alone in our house hasn't been easy. Now that I have Winston,

I'm hoping this fall and winter will be easier"

"I was thankful to have Hank. I'm sure Winston will be good company for you."

"Who's Hank?"

"He was an older lab that came into Seattle Humane Society and into my office as a client," Mike responded. "He entered my life after Elizabeth died, and he stayed with me through all the rough times. He came with me to Compassion Ranch, and the sanctuary is his final resting place."

Tears came to Erin's eyes. "A lot of loss," she said in a quiet voice.

Mike gave her a brief smile and responded, "Loss is a part of life, whether human or animal. But loss doesn't have to define us. There's so much to do and experience. I think both of our spouses would want us to remember that."

Silence passed between them for a moment. Regaining her composure, Erin said, "I'm sure you're right. Daniel continues to take care of me and the kids in many ways. He made sure the house was paid off before he retired and there is a trust fund set up for them when they each turn twenty-six. Between his military pension, death benefits, and the investments we made, I'm not having to work, although I'm considering going back to online teaching a few days a week. I want to give back, to bless others as I've been blessed, and help those in need. I'm able to do that because of Daniel's forward thinking and his dedication to his family, even though he's gone."

"We were both blessed," Mike said in a low tone. "I just wish I would have recognized my blessing sooner."

Erin squeezed his hand, still enclosed around hers. Mike looked at her and returned the gesture.

# Chapter 8

**THIRTY MINUTES** later, as Mike took grain to the horse stalls, he heard Erin's gentle voice speaking to Hope, the three-legged lamb, from the opposite side of the barn.

"You're a sweet soul, aren't you, Hope? I'm so glad you ended up here with Mike, Maggie, and the other staff. You may be getting a buddy soon, but meantime, would you like to meet Winston? He's a sweet soul, too, aren't you boy?"

Mike smiled at the conversation. As he added the oats to Cisco's feed trough, his mind travelled back thirty-two years to the after-graduation party for Clark High School outside Spokane, Washington. He and Erin sat at a table drinking sodas while music resounded throughout the pizza place's back room. High school seniors danced or stood around other tables chatting. Mike tried to talk above the noise.

"I guess we won't be seeing each other after this," he said to Erin, who was dressed in a flowery peasant top and her best blue jeans.

"I plan to stay a few months and work on Grams' and Grandpop's farm," she responded. "So,

I'll be around until the first of August anyway."

"I'm moving to Seattle next week, remember? I'm starting summer school, getting a jump on my general studies classes," he said.

"I forgot about that. The year went by fast, especially the past few months."

He took her hand. "I wish I'd gotten to know you sooner. Five months hasn't been enough time."

"I feel the same way," she whispered.

He looked into her eyes and leaned in and kissed her lips. He loved the feel of her mouth on his and his next statement was as close as he came to a proposal. "Why don't you come to Seattle? You don't know anyone in Boise so why not attend the University of Washington?"

"Scholarships. My grandparents attended Boise State and so did my parents. Because of my circumstances, losing Mom and Dad as we did, I'm still considered a resident, and I'm the daughter and granddaughter of alumni. It's the cost factor, Mike. I've told you that."

He nodded. "I'm going to miss you," he whispered.

"I'll miss you, too," she had said.

Shaking his head to release the memories, Mike patted Cisco's side and told his trusty friend,

"Sleep well, old buddy. You're going to have some new neighbors tomorrow, and it might be a little loud for several days."

Mike walked around the buckskin and closed the stall door. As he approached the opposite side of the barn where Erin was spending time with Hope, the scene before him caused him to stop. Inside the lamb's enclosure sat Erin, the young sheep's head on her lap. She stroked the animal's side. Curled up in the hay beside Hope lay Winston, the little dog's head resting against one of the lamb's front legs. Erin's closed eyes added to the peaceful scene. Mike could not avert his eyes. His heart melted at the sweetness, compassion, and love he witnessed.

Walking as quietly as possible, he approached. Winston, like many dogs protective of their owners, opened his eyes and gave a soft woof. Erin also opened her eyes. She smiled slightly, and he returned the gesture.

"Looks like you might stay in Hope's stall tonight," he commented.

"No, but I'm comfortable."

Mike leaned on the wooden fence. "Hope looks comfortable, too. So does Winston." He smiled. "I can give you a pillow if you want to bed down with the lamb tonight."

He watched Erin stroke Hope's side again. "She's a sweetie," Erin said.

He nodded. "She is that."

Mike opened the gate, and Hope started. She looked at him and bleated. Mike laughed.

"I don't know if she's saying 'hello' or scolding me for disturbing her, and you," he said.

He helped the lamb stand, and once she was steady on her three feet, he let go. Mike reached over to Erin, offering his hand. She took it and allowed him to help her rise. Erin brushed hay from her clothes and her hair. However, he noticed she missed a strand. He reached his hand toward her face.

"Here. You missed some."

He slowly removed some hay from her soft black hair. Their eyes locked. He dipped his face toward hers and, just as they had done a few times during the last few months of high school, their lips came together in a blissful, gentle, lengthy kiss. Mike relished the sweetness of the moment. A small sigh escaped, and he realized that came from him.

ERIN HEARD the sound that escaped from Mike's mouth, even with his lips sealed over hers. She attempted a step back, but the wooden fence, and Mike's body, ensnared her. So did the feelings which resurrected. The only man who had kissed her in more than twenty-five years had been Daniel. *He hasn't even been gone two years and look at yourself*, Erin's brain raged. She pulled her mouth from Mike's. Immediately warmth drained from her. She placed her hands on Mike's brawny shoulders.

"I'm sorry, Erin," he whispered. "I shouldn't have done that. I just...I'm just so attracted to you and seeing you here, so filled with compassion and grace, your loveliness just shines. I'm drawn to you like I haven't been to anyone since I lost Elizabeth."

"You're so sweet, Mike, I just don't know what to say. Except I..." Her hands dropped to her sides. "Daniel's been gone less than two years. I'm still processing..."

"I completely understand. That's why I'm apologizing."

He backtracked toward the gate and held it open for her. "Here, let's step out and talk for a bit."

Erin gave one more pat to Hope before stepping out of the enclosure. She walked to a whining Winston, untied the dog's leash from the post, and picked him up into her arms. She carried him through the open barn door and stopped near the corral. Erin gazed at the sky, filled with twinkling stars. A full moon overhead shone like the sun upon the landscape, topping the nearby mountains with golden glitter. Shadows of pine trees fell upon the landscape. The quiet of the night enveloped her and the attraction toward Mike danced within the landscape and entangled within her heart, beckoning her to join subtle music. Erin sighed. She sensed his presence beside her.

"Beautiful night," he whispered.

"Yes, it is," she responded.

Erin set Winston near her feet and turned to Mike. "I know we have feelings for each other, and we share a common tragedy. I'm just not sure I'm ready to leave Daniel's memory behind right now."

Mike placed gentle hands upon her shoulders and looked into her eyes. "I do understand, Erin, believe me. I don't want you to feel you're betraying Daniel nor am I asking you to forget him. The two of you shared many years together; Elizabeth and I did, too. I won't ever forget her. Just as I needed time to accept her passing, you need time to accept Daniel's. I guess what I want you to know is…I loved you when we were in high school. I missed you every day those first few years, and I never forgot you. I let you go because I knew we were both young, but I really didn't want to let you go."

"Why didn't you tell me then how you felt?"

He sighed and glanced to the sky before returning his gaze to her face. "I tried. I did ask you to come to Seattle, if you remember."

She nodded. "I remember. But all you said was you wanted me to come to Seattle; you didn't say why or that you loved me."

"I wanted to, but I listened to my dad and my best friend and kept my feelings bottled up. I focused on my schooling and my career. I made a mistake by not being truthful about loving you. I didn't know what happened to you, where you were, but I looked for you at our fifth high school reunion. I thought if I saw you there, I could tell you how I felt and maybe we could try again. But you weren't there."

She shook her head. "I was planning my wedding then and since I had only attended high school that one year, I didn't have the inclination to go." She stared into his eyes. "I actually thought I'd hear from you that first year of college. I did wait, Mike, but by my sophomore year, I figured you weren't interested after all, and I moved on."

"To Daniel."

She shook her head. "Not at first, but I began dating. I met Daniel the start of spring semester. By summer, after meeting each other's families, we were serious. I figured you had moved on, too."

He nodded. "I dated a bit, but my feelings for you didn't subside. I didn't try to find you because … well, my parents kept pushing me to do well in school and get into vet school and launch my career. I regret listening to them, and not my heart."

He placed his hands on her face and looked deeply into her eyes. "I still love you, Erin, and now that we've reconnected, I want you to know I'm here for you. Whenever you feel ready, I'll be here. We can stay in touch, visit each other now and then, and see what happens. Maybe you'll come to love me, maybe you won't. I'm okay with that. I'm not going anywhere. But, if nothing else, you can know you have a good friend, even a special companion if you want. I'm here."

Her eyes searched his, and she saw honesty and integrity…and love. She lay her head on his shoulder and felt him wrap his arm around her waist while his other hand cupped her face. Warmth returned, and she sighed.

# Chapter 9

**AT 6:30** the next morning, Erin spoke to her sister on the phone.

"I'm glad I didn't wake you. I hardly slept last night," Erin confessed.

"You know Levi and I are early risers, having the rescue and all," Rhiann said.

"That's why I didn't call last night. I needed time to think anyway."

"Still processing things about Mike?"

"He kissed me last night, Rhiann."

"Oh." A few seconds of silence passed before she continued, "How did you feel about that?"

"Conflicted."

"Understandable." Erin sensed her sister nod. Another few seconds of silence passed, and then Rhiann asked, "Do you remember telling me what you and Daniel talked about before his passing?"

"Yeah...Yes..." Erin stretched the words out, not wanting to revisit that conversation.

She realized her sister sensed her hesitation when Rhiann said, "You're not betraying Daniel, Erin. He gave you his blessing to find love again. You're only fifty-three years old."

"Daniel was only fifty-five when he died."

Erin's comeback was meant to make a different point than what her younger sister interpreted, for Rhiann said, "That's my point. One never knows the future. That's why Daniel told you to not grieve for him too long, that you have a life to live, however long that is. He wanted, and all of us want, you to have a long life, a happy life."

Erin pondered her sister's words. After a moment, Rhiann's voice came back across the line. "Erin? Are you there?"

"Yes, I'm here. I have more thinking to do, I believe."

"Take your time. If Mike is a decent guy, he'll let you have your space so you can sort things out and take the path that's best for you."

"He is a decent guy. He even told me if friendship is all I want, he's okay with that. But Rhiann, he said he's always loved me. What am I to do with that?"

"Be grateful. Not everyone is blessed with the love of two good men in their lives. Daniel loved you, Erin, but, like many, he also loved his career, and sometimes he loved that more, I think. That happens. Now, here you've re-met Mike, a guy who enjoys what he does, knows he makes a difference, but is open to giving you his love, a love he's held onto for years. You're fortunate. Maybe the timing isn't right exactly now, but perhaps in six months it will be. If he's willing to wait as you continue to grieve for Daniel, I'd say go for it. Knowing you'll have someone there for you as you continue this journey is an amazing gift."

Erin didn't speak for a moment. When she did, she allowed gratitude and love for her sister to pour forth. "You're right. Thank you, sis. I appreciate your listening ear and your advice. I'm grateful to you and Levi for all you've done for me and the kids since Daniel died. I know you're right when you say Daniel wanted me to be happy; he did tell me so several times during that last month. I just didn't even want to think about it; I find it still hard to think about life without him."

"Like I said, take your time. Mike's a great guy to tell you the same thing."

Erin smiled. "Yes, he's a great guy."

THAT AFTERNOON, as Erin played with the cats, she focused again on the two yellow tabby brothers, Ricky and Rocket. The more she engaged with them, the more certain she was that her daughter would enjoy these kitties. She watched Rocket refocus his attention on a sunbeam dancing across the nearby wall. She laughed as the tabby leaped, as if trying to catch the light. Another sunray on the floor captured his interest, and the cat began zooming around the room. With her cell phone, Erin snapped several pictures of Ricky playing with a catnip mouse and others of Rocket pouncing on rays of sunlight.

A few moments later she texted the photos to Brittany along with this message: "I think I've found the purr-fect cats for you! Two brothers, about two years old. Playful, fun, and friendly. We already know they get along, they are healthy, and they like people. What do you think? Want me to adopt them for you?"

As she waved a feather toy in front of the tabbies' faces, Brittany responded with a text: "YES! I already love them. Do they get along with Winston?"

Erin responded, "I'll plan a sleep-over to find out. Potential adopters can do that here, just like at Best Friends Animal Society."

"Super!" came Brittany's response. "Let me know how everyone does."

Just then, Leslie, the animal caregiver, dashed in with a large grin on her face. "The new beagles have arrived! Want to come see them?"

Looking up, Erin smiled back. She stood up and responded, "Of course! Lead the way."

MIKE STOOD on the outside of a group of small stalls in the barn, constructed to hold the new canine arrivals. Ten beagles, ranging from young adults to aging seniors, either sat staring or walked around their enclosure, sniffing and exploring. The three that sat quivered.

Standing beside Mike, observing the newest sanctuary residents, Maggie whispered, "Looks like we have three on the more nervous side."

Mike nodded. "Three of ten—not bad."

"How do they seem temperament-wise?"

"All will be adoptable. No behavior issues with this group. The three that are trembling will likely take the most work. I doubt they were handled much except for the experimentation. These other seven – none were aggressive and, since they are younger, probably weren't exposed as much to the pharmaceutical testing procedures as the three older ones. I think they'll all be adoptable eventually."

Leslie and Erin walked into the barn. Maggie and Mike glanced over when they heard the door open and waited for the two women to join them. Leslie's large smile graced her face.

"Aren't they adorable?" she commented to no one in particular.

Erin stood next to Maggie and soaked in the sight without a response. Mike watched her for a moment, wondering what she was thinking.

"Leslie, I'll have you work with Mike caring for these dogs while we still have Erin, Jordan, and Lauren here the next few days," Maggie instructed. "The sooner we can handle these dogs and get them used to people not causing them pain, the sooner they become adoptable."

"I'm here for another week, so as much as I can help, I will," Erin said in a soft voice.

"We appreciate that, Erin. You've come at a really good time. The cats should be here in two days, so that gives us a good start with the beagles," Maggie said.

Erin looked at Maggie. "Why beagles?"

The sanctuary's director looked at Mike.

"They're gentle creatures and don't usually

become aggressive," he responded. "Also, they will eat even if they don't feel good. So, they're reliable as research animals."

Erin looked at the three staff members. "I'm glad you're here. I'm glad I'm here."

*Me, too,* Mike thought as he studied the compassion on her face.

# Chapter 10

**ERIN SAT** on her porch eating chicken salad for lunch the next afternoon; Winston lay on his blanket beside her. She heard laughter and the cabin door across the way open and close. She looked over and smiled at Lauren and Jordan as they walked across the wooden porch of their small log lodge.

"Hi, you two!" she said and waved at them.

Both looked her way and waved back. As they walked toward her, Erin rose from her chair, meeting them part-way.

"We don't mean to disturb your lunch," Jordan said.

"No problem. How's your day going?"

"Great! We think we're going to adopt one of the beagles," Lauren said.

"One of the new ones?"

Lauren shook her head. "No, they're not ready, and might not be for a while, according to Maggie. We've been spending some time with Riley, the light tri-colored three-year-old. He's so sweet!"

"Oh, yes, I agree."

"We're having a sleep-over with him tonight to see how he and Molly get along," Lauren said.

Erin's smile grew wider. "Winston and I are having a sleep-over tonight, too...with two cats."

Jordan grinned. "Pet parties at the cabins!"

The two women laughed.

"Two cats? Wow!" Lauren said.

"They're for my daughter. She'll be graduating college at the end of the year, and she wants to start her new chapter of life with some cuddly creatures. A dog would likely be too much for her, starting her career, but two cats will be company for her and for each other when she's working."

"What does she plan to do?" Jordan asked.

"She's studying marine biology and she'd like to work for a conservation organization. She interned at Sea World last year during the summer and she's volunteered with a sea turtle rescue group for the past three years."

"Sound like amazing experiences," Lauren commented.

Erin nodded. "She really enjoyed them. Jobs...well, that can be another matter."

A moment of silence passed between them.

"So which two cats have you chosen for your sleep-over?" Jordan asked.

"The two light gold tabby brothers, Ricky and Rocket," Erin responded.

"Oh, they're delightful!" Lauren commented.

Erin smiled. "Yes, they are. Older but still playful."

Lauren laughed. "Especially Rocket! I can see why they named him that."

Erin chuckled. "So true! They're obviously bonded, which is great. If they get along with Winston, I think they'll be perfect for Brittany."

"Well, we'd best get on down to the barn. We're helping Leslie and Maggie this afternoon clean up after the new dogs."

Erin nodded. "And I'm up to the Kitty Castle to play with cats and bring two back here later in the day."

"Have a good one," Jordan said as he and Lauren stepped off the porch.

"You, too." Erin waved at them and then returned to her chair.

She picked up her bowl and Winston jumped

into her lap. He sniffed her food dish then turned up his nose. Erin laughed.

"I keep trying to tell you all people food isn't dog food, but no—you have to be nosey, don't you?"

She hugged him with her right arm and placed her cheek against his. In a soft voice, she added, "Our life, my life, that is, is going to be quite different from here on out, Winston. "Although my children are in Florida, I'm returning to an empty house. I'm glad you'll be there, and I do hope Ricky and Rocket will be with us as well. This big change in my life will be a lot easier with you and the cats there."

Winston licked her face and, after one more hug to her dog, Erin stared at the vast landscape beyond the cabin's porch.

MIKE CANTERED Cisco from the back woods after finding the five Belgian horses deep in the forest. He couldn't blame them for seeking shade on this hot early August afternoon. Yet, he had been troubled to not find them in the large pasture. Rarely had they left the big, grassy range the entire summer. At least he had coaxed them closer to a clearing.

With mountain lions and grizzly bears roaming the area, he preferred seeing them on the edge of the woods, not deep in the forest. Of course, they could roam wherever they wanted, but having such a large space for livestock created risk from predators. That was part of being here and tending to livestock. All the staff knew they could lose an animal to predators even though they tried their best to not let that happen. Mike looked forward to the coolness of autumn when even the horses would stay in pastures closer to the barn.

He would ride back up here later in the afternoon and try to bring the Belgians to the lower pasture for the evening, maybe even corral them near the barn for the night. He needed to vaccinate all the livestock in the coming days so having the horses nearby would make that job a lot easier.

Meantime, he was on a mission. He'd come to a decision and now was riding Cisco toward the guest cabins. He thought he'd be able to catch up with Erin before she conducted her afternoon volunteer duties.

He reined Cisco to a stop at Erin's cabin, dismounted, and tied the buckskin to a porch post. He watched Erin close and lock the door. She startled when she looked up.

"Oh! I didn't hear you."

"Sorry. I didn't mean to scare you. I just rode Cisco in from the woods."

He nodded toward the forest. Erin walked closer, meeting him on the porch steps.

"How was your morning?" Mike asked.

"Good. I was with the dogs this morning, and now I'm heading to the Kitty Castle."

"I'll walk with you if that's okay."

"Sure."

Mike untied Cisco as Erin walked down the steps. They strolled side-by-side from the cabin area toward the pets' lodging quarters, the buckskin horse trailing behind Mike as the ranch manager held the reins.

"Maggie and Leslie are getting the new dogs settled in," Mike said.

Erin nodded. "I visited a bit with Lauren and Jordan. They said they would be working with the new dogs today, helping the ladies."

"I think most of them will adapt well. That's good because it's not always the case."

"I never fully realized the extent of research on animals."

"Most people don't. We humans just don't think about it. I knew more because of my veterinary practice and my time at vet school."

Erin looked at him. "Is it hard? Going from vet practice to working here?"

Mike shook his head. "No. Although I had to accept it as a vet student and practicing clinician, I always felt bad most of the animals were euthanized after the research. Being here now, well, it's my way of giving back, of taking care of the animals that endure so much on behalf of humankind … and their own kind. It's a good thing that Compassion Ranch, and places like it, now exist."

"I feel the same way."

He looked at her and then put a gentle hand on her arm. They both stopped walking. Erin looked into his eyes.

"Is something wrong?"

Mike gave her a wobbly smile. "No, no nothing's wrong. I wanted to…that is, if you'd like to, I'd enjoy taking you into town tonight and having dinner with you."

He watched her face as she pondered his invitation.

"I think…I believe I'd enjoy that, too."

Mike smiled. "I'll pick you up at 6:30."

She nodded, and they continued to walk toward the animal buildings.

"I had planned to do a sleep over with Ricky and Rocket tonight, but that can wait," Erin said.

"We'll pick them up when we get back. Might take two people anyway."

She nodded. "Maggie gave me tomorrow off to spend time with them and with Winston, so if you're okay with that, I'd appreciate the help later."

"No trouble at all."

They arrived at the Kitty Castle. Mike smiled at her once again and said, "I'll see you this evening at 6:30."

She gave him a tentative smile. "That you will. Have a good afternoon."

He nodded and said, "Thanks. You, too."

Mike swung his body into the saddle atop Cisco. He touched the brim of his cowboy hat before reining the horse toward the office building. He felt his heart enlarge, and he let out a deep breath. *Well, that went better than I thought.* He steeled his wits to concentrate again on work, and when he arrived at the administration building, he dismounted from Cisco and walked inside. Kaitlyn looked up from her desk.

"Hey, Kate," Mike greeted her. "I need to see the last prescription and vaccine orders. I want to make sure we have what we need for the sheep, cows, and horses."

"Sure thing. I'll get those."

"Is Maggie in?"

Just then, the director peered her face around her office door.

"She sure is. Come on in," Maggie responded. Mike obliged. "Did you find the Belgians?"

He nodded. "They were in the forest near the high pasture. I'm going to try to bring them down later this afternoon and secure them near the barn."

"Need an extra hand?"

He smiled. "I was hoping you'd offer. I plan to go up around three. That work for you?"

She nodded. "I'll be ready."

Kaitlyn brought in a folder of order forms and receipts and gave them to Mike. He smiled at her as he took the file from her hands. "Thanks."

She nodded. "Last month's orders are in there, too. The payment is set to go out this week along with other bills to be paid."

"Thanks, Kate."

The young woman left the office. As he opened the file, Maggie's low voice asked, "So, how's it going with Erin?"

He looked up. "What do you mean?"

Maggie smiled. "I heard the back story – you two knew each other in high school. I've seen the way you look at her. That first love never left you, did it?"

Crimson climbed into his cheeks. He lowered his voice. "Shows that much, does it?"

"Only to those who might be curious, like me." Maggie took a deep breath. "I'm happy for you, Mike, both of you. Each of you lost a spouse and had a friendship that can be rekindled, maybe grow into something special. I hope all works out. You and Erin deserve happiness and love."

"Yeah, well, her loss was more recent. I have to tread carefully."

"Hard to do?"

He nodded. "Sometimes. We are going out to dinner tonight. That's another reason I came to see you, to let you know Erin and I will be off-site for a few hours." Maggie nodded. "I'll also help her bring the two cats she's interested in up to her cabin when we get back."

Maggie nodded again. "Sounds good. I gave her tomorrow off to spend with the boys."

"She mentioned that."

"Going to be hard to see her leave."

He nodded and sighed. "Yeah, that it is. I also want to take her to the Buffalo Bill Museum. We'd need to be off on the same day."

He realized he didn't ask Maggie's permission. With so little time, he wasn't going to ask. He hoped Maggie would understand. The two looked each other in the eye.

"With all these animals coming in, including horses you have to go and pick up, that might be hard to wrangle, Mike," Maggie said.

He nodded. "Think you could ask Jordan and Lauren to stay another day?"

Maggie shook her head. "They have reservations in both Yellowstone and Glacier. Those can't be broken." Maggie's face lit up. "Maybe Gary's available. You remember that Forest Service seasonal worker who was here in June. He told me to contact him whenever we have need for an extra hand, and if he's available, he said he'd help. I'll call him and see."

"Great idea. Let me know as soon as you hear from him."

"Maybe we can get Erin to stay a bit longer."

"You can ask," Mike responded.

His heart whispered a silent prayer that Erin would say *yes*.

# Chapter 11

**LATER THAT** evening, Erin and Mike sat across from one another in a booth inside Sadie Mae's, a Cody restaurant. Log walls with large windows surrounded them. Erin glanced around as she unfolded a white linen napkin onto her lap.

"Very western," she commented.

"With very good food," Mike said. She looked at him. "It's popular with both residents and tourists, known for its steak, prime rib, and chicken dishes." He grinned. "I thought it would appeal to both our palates."

Erin smiled. A waitress stopped at their booth and inquired, "May I get you something to drink before you order?"

Mike looked at Erin. "Would you like a glass of wine?"

"Actually, yes. Do you have Kendall-Jackson Chardonnay?"

"We do," the young blonde server replied.

Erin smiled. "A glass of that, please."

"Certainly. Sir?"

"I'll have a Sam Adams Summer Ale."

"I'll bring those out."

As the waitress left, Erin turned her attention back to Mike. "So, tell me about the veterinary clinic you had in Seattle."

"The practice was a great success," Mike responded. "I enjoyed the work, had great clients, and I was able to help several of Seattle's local rescues and animal shelters. I helped start a second low-cost spay-neuter clinic, with several of my veterinary colleagues. We took turns – once a month one of us would host and cover the clinic."

"That's wonderful! I wish more vets would do such things."

He nodded. "Of course we lose money, that's why the sharing is vital. However, when animal shelters and rescues are filled to capacity and litters of puppies and kittens make up a huge percentage of those numbers, I believe we have a duty to help not only the rescues through such clinics, but our clients as well so they don't contribute to the problem."

"I know my sister and her contacts have tried to get such a program going in Montana, but only a few towns offer it."

Mike nodded again. "Whenever I've spoken at conferences, I've made a pitch for low-cost spay/neuter programs. It was a tough sell early on, but I know there are pockets of such programs in parts of the country."

"When I get back to Florida, I plan to contact veterinary clinics and see if I can help start more programs in the state," Erin said. "I've learned so much from Rhiann these past several months. I wasn't into the animal rescue like she was, and still is, but spending time at her sanctuary, and now here, I see the vital need."

AFTER ORDERING their meals, Mike asked Erin, "Did you ever go back to Boise after you and Daniel married?"

Erin shook her head. "We travelled so much during his early career, and after Rhiann returned to Washington to care for our grandparents, there wasn't a reason to."

"I assume you visited them in Spokane occasionally."

Erin nodded. "Off and on. Rhiann and Grams spent some time in Arizona after Grandpop died. I'd visit there now and then."

Mike looked into her eyes. "I wish we'd have stayed in touch. I would have liked to have seen you again, perhaps gotten a coffee when we were both in Spokane."

Erin detected sorrow in his voice.

"Mike, we can't turn back time. We followed our college plans and we met our spouses. We each have great kids. There's no reason to rehash 'what ifs.'"

He nodded. "I know. Sometimes, though, I wish I had made different choices."

"Why?" She locked her eyes on his. "You enjoyed a successful veterinary practice, lived in a beautiful city, married a wonderful woman, as I understand, and you have two amazing kids. I experienced many of the same joys. We each had blessed lives."

He smiled. "That's one of the things I remember about you, one of the things that drew me to you back in high school—your positive outlook on life."

"My Grams taught me that. When Rhiann and I lost our parents, we both felt our world had crumbled down around us. Grams had lost her son, my father—she grieved and she let us grieve, but she also kept reminding us to not live in sorrow, to look for the beauty in life and the blessings we still had. Grams and Grandpop were among those blessings."

Silence passed between them, and then the waitress brought their dinners. The young woman asked, "May I get anything else for you right now?"

Erin and Mike looked at one another.

"I'm good," Erin said.

Mike smiled at their server. "I think we're fine for now, thank you."

She smiled back. "Let me know if you need anything. Enjoy your meals."

As the waitress walked away, Erin looked at her plate of chicken breast with lemon and rosemary sauce with a side of asparagus.

"This looks delicious," she commented.

"They make fine food here," Mike said.

He began to cut the piece of London broil on his plate.

Erin observed him relish the bite. "Good?" she asked.

He nodded and smiled. "This is one of their specialties. I generally have it when I stop here."

Erin cut into her chicken and took a small bite. She savored the tanginess and juiciness of the meat and smiled.

"Yours good, too?" Mike asked.

She nodded, the smile still on her face. "Tastes as good as it looks and smells."

Quiet settled between them as they ate several bites of food. Mike prompted conversation again by asking, "So you said you weren't much into animal rescue until recently, but being with Rhiann changed that?"

Erin nodded. "Because Daniel and I moved so much, and I did work and raise the kids, my primary focus was on family. I did rescue a duck once, many years ago."

"A duck? How'd that come about?"

Erin chuckled at the surprise in Mike's tone. "I know that sounds strange, but it's true. I was taking a walk one afternoon near a lake when I noticed a young female mallard duck. She looked sick, and when I got closer, I noticed her feet tangled in algae. I picked her up and cleaned her off with some wipes that I had in my pocket. She was so weak; she didn't even fight me. I wasn't sure she'd even survive, but after untangling her and cleaning her off, I set her back into the water in a spot away from the algae. She perked up almost immediately. She floated at first, then began paddling. In just a few minutes her strength returned, and I watched her swim off. My first rescue, and I was able to save an animal's life!"

Her large smile helped convey her excitement. Mike smiled back.

"A person doesn't forget the first life they save, human or animal."

Erin leaned closer to him. "I imagine you've saved a lot of lives. Tell me about your first."

Mike grinned. "I had adopted a lab named Jake. He became our office dog. One day he got into something in the alley that caused a seizure and he stopped breathing. That was the first time I ever did mouth to snout resuscitation. Not the last time, but the first time."

"I've heard the Red Cross offers pet first aid and CPR classes."

Mike nodded. "Comes in handy sometimes."

"Rhiann and her husband have both taken the course. She offered to send me, but the timing wasn't right. Now that I have Winston, though, I think when I get back to Florida, I'll sign up for a class."

"I can teach you," Mike said, looking into her eyes. "That way in case something was to happen while you're on your trip back home, you'll have some knowledge of what to do."

Erin's body shuddered, thinking about the possibility of needing such information so soon. Mike must have noticed. He reached a hand across the table and clasped one of hers.

"Not saying anything will happen, but just in case. Best to be prepared."

Erin cocked her head, looking back at him. "How did you know what I was thinking?"

He smiled. "Intuition. I've worked with thousands of pet parents, remember?"

She smiled back and withdrew her hand. His touch aroused feelings she didn't want to experience, and though she deciphered he meant comfort, she knew she needed to squelch other feelings which rose within her. Erin returned to her meal. So did Mike.

"Let's see if there's time for that," Erin said. "I do appreciate the offer."

"Speaking of, I think Maggie wants to ask you to stay a bit longer," Mike said.

His statement caught her off-guard and she looked at him.

"Oh? Why?"

"With Lauren and Jordan leaving, she thinks we need an extra hand to help socialize the new dogs."

"I really do need to get back," Erin stated. "It will take me close to a week to drive home, and my kids are getting ready to return to school. I want to spend some time with them before that; it's been a few months since I've seen them."

Mike nodded. "I understand. Perhaps a just

few days more? We can use the help."

"Are you sure? You all have done so much without me or other volunteers in the past."

"Yes, we make do, but if there's a possibility of an extra hand, it's always welcome."

We'll see," Erin responded in a quiet voice.

They returned to their meal.

INWARDLY, MIKE kicked himself. *I should have left that up to Maggie*, he mused in his brain. *After taking her hand a moment ago, I should just have left that conversation alone. She's not interested in me, and I just need to let this go, let her go.*

His fingers still tingled from enfolding her hand into his. *How can I let her go a second time?* His heart shredded at the conflicting thoughts and the war waged within him about next steps. He startled at the buzzing from his cell phone. Mike picked up the device from his pocket, glanced at the number and frowned. Erin must have noticed his expression for she asked, "What's wrong?"

"It's Maggie," he said, and he answered the call. "Hey, Maggie. What's up?"

"I'm sorry to bother you," came her response, "but the pregnant ewe has gone into labor, and she's having problems."

"We'll be right there!"

He clicked off, looked at Erin, and simultaneously took his wallet from his back pocket. As he withdrew a one-hundred-dollar bill and placed it on the table, he explained to Erin, "The pregnant ewe's in labor, and Maggie said the birth isn't going well. We have to get back."

"Of course!"

Mike stood and assisted Erin from the booth. Upon reaching the restaurant door, he held it open for her and followed her outside to his truck. He opened the passenger side door and closed it after she climbed into the seat. Mike rushed around the front of the vehicle and jumped into the driver's side. After backing from the parking space, he put the truck in DRIVE and headed the vehicle out of town, attempting to stay within the speed limit. He worried his lower lip, his brain awhirl with thoughts of how to help the ewe when they arrived back at the sanctuary.

# Chapter 12

**ERIN WATCHED** as Mike spoke in a soothing, quiet voice to the mama sheep as she labored to deliver the lamb within her. She sat in the stall with the ewe's head on her lap stroking the animal's forehead, and Leslie sat nearby, massaging the sheep's stomach. Mike squatted behind the animal, coaxing the breached baby from within the mama. Maggie stood nearby with numerous rags in hand.

Erin tried to focus on calming and comforting the laboring sheep as the ewe panted and heaved. She couldn't help but listen to Mike's encouraging words, as if the poor creature could understand. Yet, her own motherly instinct believed the sheep knew he was trying to help, that they all were trying to help. Despite the mother's physical pain, the ewe did what all mothers do at this time—deliver her baby.

"Got it!" Mike said, a happy note to his voice. Erin looked at him. He still concentrated his attention to the sheep's birthing. "The lamb's leg is out of the way, so now we can help this mom give birth and bring this little one into the world."

He moved into a different position. "Maggie,

hand me a couple of those rags and get ready to catch while I help her expel the rest of the fluid."

At that moment, the ewe gave one big push and Erin watched a black-spotted lamb drop into the bed of hay near Mike. Maggie reached out and grabbed the newborn, wrapping it in large cloths. Mike and Leslie began to massage the mom and Erin refocused on the ewe as she tried to stand.

"Keep her down another minute, Erin," she heard Mike say. "We have some clean-up work to do back here."

Erin continued her soothing voice as she spoke to the sheep and stroked the animal's head. "You're a good girl. You have a beautiful baby you'll see very soon."

"Okay, Erin, let her up now," Mike said.

The ewe wiggled from Erin's grasp and, on lamb-like wobbly legs, stood up. Erin remained seated, putting her hands out to catch the sheep in case she toppled over. A few seconds later, hearing her lamb bleat, the ewe turned around. Erin watched the new mother lovingly caress her youngster. With Maggie's help, the lamb meandered toward the sheep's backend and latched on. The newborn nursed as if famished. Laughter and smiles broke out in the stall. A smile on her own face, Erin stood and watched Mike, Maggie, and Leslie high-five one another. Mike glanced her way with a large grin and a twinkle in his eyes.

AN HOUR later, Mike and Erin strolled side-by-side along the gravel road near the barn. Winston trotted on Erin's left, and Mike walked on the right.

"Your help was greatly appreciated at the barn tonight," Mike said in a low tone.

"I didn't do anything but cradle her."

"That helped keep her calm, which is important," he stated.

"I can see the good you do here, Mike, not only as ranch manager, but being a veterinarian. You saved both the mother and the baby."

"Sometimes that's not always possible, but we were lucky."

They walked in silence for a short time.

"By the way, Maggie didn't have an opportunity to tell you, but she's giving you and me a day off together in two days. We can go to the historical center."

Erin looked at him. "But the dogs...and you all have cats coming in."

He nodded. "And horses. She's got a young Forest Service worker coming in to help while we're in town. That is, if you want to go."

Erin smiled. "Yes, I'd like to go."

Mike smiled in return. "Wonderful. Winston can stay with Maggie and Kaitlyn at the office. He'll get walks and lots of spoiling."

Erin laughed. She stopped and stooped down to pat her dog's head. "Hear that, boy? Lots of spoiling!"

The Cavalier let out a happy yip. Mike and Erin chuckled and began strolling with the dog again.

"Thanks for letting me walk with you and Winston," Mike said. "I'm usually pretty wound up after something like that, and I appreciate the company. But it's late. You should get back to your cabin."

"Winston needed the walk, and truthfully, so do I. I haven't been involved in an animal's birth before. I admit, I held my breath a lot."

Mike grinned. "So did I."

She stopped and looked at him. "You did? I thought you'd be an old hat at that kind of stuff."

"I am, but that doesn't mean when things get especially hectic, I don't get a bit nervous. I never want to lose an animal, but I recognize the possibility. Yet, I do everything I can to prevent it, and that sometimes means whispering a prayer and holding my breath."

Their eyes locked for a moment, and upon continuing their stroll, Erin whispered, "I wonder if human doctors do the same?"

Recognizing she was probably thinking about her deceased husband, Mike captured her hand in his and squeezed it.

"I imagine many do," he said in a low voice.

Mike noticed the crescent moon dangling over a nearby hillside.

"Look at that," he said.

Erin cast her eyes skyward and smiled. "I love watching the moon. Whenever we're at the ocean, the moon rise and its brightness are incredible! But I've found out west that such a sight is also amazing."

Mike watched her a moment and felt his heart quicken. He bit his lower lip and returned his gaze at the night sky. As he squeezed her hand, he whispered, "Yes, truly amazing."

# Chapter 13

**THE NEXT** morning, about mid-day, Erin stood at the cabin's kitchen sink. As she rinsed her coffee cup, she gazed out the window. Her neighbor's car was no longer parked across the gravel lot. She wished she had been able to say goodbye to the young couple before they left and regretted not exchanging contact information with them. They were people with whom she'd like to stay in contact.

As she pondered these thoughts, Mike's pickup came to a halt alongside her cabin. Erin watched as he opened the driver's side door and jumped to the ground. Erin's heart summersaulted and thundered in her chest. She sighed. *Do I really have to feel this way?* She flexed and then rubbed her right hand, remembering the comfort and warmth from last night as she and Mike held hands. She picked up a towel as a knock sounded on the wooden front door.

Erin glanced at Winston, lying on a turquoise dog bed in the living room. Her furry friend's head rose at the sound.

"Stay!" Erin commanded him as she

approached the cabin door. Upon opening it, Mike's dashing smile greeted her.

"Morning."

She returned his grin. "Good morning to you. Come in for coffee? I still have some left."

"That would be great," he responded, and she widened the entrance for him. Mike stepped inside and pulled a piece of paper from his shirt pocket. "I have something for you."

Erin accepted the page. "What is it?"

"A note from Lauren. She and Jordan left about two hours ago. I guess she tapped on your door, but you didn't answer."

"Oh, dear! I never heard her knock."

With another smile, he responded, "No surprise. Staying up until midnight with a sheep in labor and then another hour or so walking with me, you needed your sleep." He followed her to the table. "You read your note, I can get the coffee."

Erin nodded and sat on one of the dining chairs. As she surveyed the handwritten missive, she heard Mike rummage in the cupboard for a coffee mug. She shut out the background noise of pouring coffee to focus on Lauren's words:

"Dear Erin: Jordan and I are sorry to have missed you before we left. We enjoyed getting to know you. Maggie informed us about the events last night—how wonderful for you to help the poor mama sheep and her little one. Thank you for your kindness toward and help with the animals at Compassion Ranch! We love this place and plan to return later this fall for another volunteer project helping with an in-person adoption event. I don't know if you can swing it, but if so, we'd love to see you here for that! Meantime let's keep in touch. Our email address is LnJGriff@yahoomail.com, and my cell phone is 970-555-1212. Have a safe trip home! – Lauren Griffith."

Erin smiled. "They want to stay in touch. I'm glad about that. Just a bit ago, I was wishing I had given them my contact information so we could keep in touch."

Mike sat on a chair opposite Erin. "That's great. They're a fine couple."

"How's their new adopted dog doing with Molly, and vice-versa?"

"Great! Everyone seems happy. Speaking of adoption, so sorry about the cats not being able to come over last night."

Erin smiled. "You mean early this morning. That's okay. Winston and I needed to sleep in today."

Mike smiled back. "Very true. Well, what do you say we go get those boys and bring them back so you and Winston can spend the day with them?"

"Don't you all need me today? With Jordan and Lauren gone…"

"Remember that Maggie gave you the day off? Besides, since today is Saturday, we have a few people coming out on a tour this afternoon; they're staying a few extra hours to volunteer. It's a family from Arizona escaping the heat."

"I assume school hasn't started for them."

Mike shook his head. "They don't start until September when the heat lessens a bit."

"Does the heat ever lessen in Arizona?"

He laughed. "I guess there are a few 'cooler' months."

"Rhiann and her husband honeymooned in Tucson. They had a Valentine's Day wedding."

Mike smiled and nodded. "Likely about the best time of year to be in Arizona."

"Or Florida," Erin said with a smile.

"Spring training for baseball in both places. Like I said, the best time of year to be there."

She cocked her head and asked, "Are you a baseball fan?"

He nodded again. "Sure am. Don't get to see

much of it in person, but I catch a game on TV here and there. When I lived in Seattle, I made it to some of the Mariners' games. Having two sons helped increase my enjoyment of the game."

"Brian loves the Rays," Erin said. "He and Daniel spent a lot of time either watching on TV or going to games, and when spring training rolled around, nearly every weekend they, or we as an entire family, would head over to the coast to catch games." She paused a moment and then whispered, "Good memories."

"That's always important," Mike responded. "I'll always have those Mariner games as memories with my boys."

A moment of silence passed between them. Mike sipped his coffee and then asked, "So, would you like to go get your potential new furry friends and bring them back to the cabin for the day? I can help before our visitors come."

"Yes, that would be great. If you and Maggie are sure you don't need me today..."

Mike shook his head. "You put in extra work with the ewe and lamb. Take some time for yourself and the animals." He grinned. "Orders from Maggie. And me."

Erin smiled back. "Okay, I will do that." She rose from the chair. "Let me run a brush through my hair and I'll be ready to go."

*YOUR HAIR looks beautiful as it is.* That thought jolted Mike's heart, and he sighed. *I have to stop this. So much of her life still revolves around Daniel. I need to step back. She still needs time to heal.*

Mike sighed again.

COMING FROM the cabin's bathroom, Erin heard his sigh. She stopped before rounding the corner to the kitchen and bit her bottom lip. She had heard that sound before when Mike didn't think she noticed or had been within ear-shot. She felt his turmoil because she also experienced that feeling. Summing up courage, Erin stepped into the kitchen.

"Mike, I think we have to talk." She noticed his eyes drilling into hers. Erin sat in the chair she had recently vacated. "I've been a widow for less than two years. I shared more than twenty-five years with Daniel and our two children. Now I'm facing a new chapter of my life and having to readjust my thinking about the future."

He nodded. "I completely understand."

"Do you, Mike?"

"I've been there, Erin, you know that."

"But you had your career. I was a wife, a military wife at that, and a mother. I worked some, yes, but my focus was my family. Now not only have I lost my husband, but my children are grown and soon will be independent adults with careers. I'm having to readjust not only because I've lost my spouse, but I'm losing my children."

He nodded. "I do understand. My sons are in college, too, remember?" He reached for her hands and covered them with his. Boring his eyes into hers, Mike whispered, "I've gone through much of the same. When Elizabeth died in that car accident, the shock didn't wear off for more than a year. I was a zombie, even at work. But I had to continue, for my sons' sakes. They were still in high school, and so I had to put one foot in front of the other and go on. It wasn't easy."

He sighed and glanced away for a few seconds before returning his gaze to Erin's face. "I want you to know that I don't want to push you, but I also want you to know I care. If you're willing to take a chance on me, I'll be there for you. I am here for you. Whatever you need. A listening ear, a shoulder to cry on, someone to hold your hand, someone to give you friendship and a hope for the future. I've loved you since high school, Erin, and though we went our separate ways and we each married someone else, you remained in my heart. Finding you here, being with you, has been and is such a joy. I feel perhaps we have a second chance. But I know your world has been turned upside down these past many months. I'm sorry you've had to go through such pain. I'm sorry you lost the man you loved. But, when you feel you're ready to try again, I want to be the man you look to for love."

Erin stared at him and saw the sincerity reflected in his eyes as well as heard it in his voice. Tears began to flow.

"How could I be so blessed to have the love of two wonderful, fine men?" she whispered.

Mike smiled and reached out a hand and wiped her tears with his thumb. He leaned close and kissed her cheek with gentle lips. He pressed his forehead onto hers.

"Because he and I know the special woman you are," he whispered.

Silence enfolded for a moment as each relished the closeness.

"I can't promise anything, Mike," Erin said in a soft voice.

"I know," he responded in a low tone.

A slight smile came to her face. "But I am enjoying this."

"Good," he said as he looked at her with a smile. "That's a start."

# Chapter 14

**SUNSHINE BLAZED** through the cabin's living room windows later that afternoon. Two male yellow tabby cats lay stretched on the couch, eyes closed, relishing the light rays saturating the piece of furniture. Erin sat in a nearby recliner, a book in her hand and Winston curled upon her lap. A knock sounded on the front door. Erin looked up and caught Maggie's eye. She motioned the sanctuary's director to come inside. Maggie obliged the signal and stepped in through the door. Erin put a finger to her lips and pointed at the cats lying on the couch. She stood, holding onto Winston, and led the way to the kitchen and then out the other door to the cabin's porch. Closing the door behind Maggie, Erin smiled.

"Sorry. That's the first time they slowed down since getting here four hours ago. I thought it best to let them sleep a bit more."

Maggie smiled back. "No problem. I'm glad to see they're doing so well. I thought they'd be hiding."

"They did the first hour. I finally coaxed them from under the bed with a few feather toys. We played in the bedroom with the door closed for a while. I brought them out and closed off the doors to the other rooms. They hid under the couch for another thirty minutes because of Winston. He was so good, though! Being at Rhiann's rescue helped him adjust to cats. The three of them played and let me join in for a time. Then the cats crashed. Winston, too, as you saw."

Maggie scratched the little dog's head. "You're going to be a good big brother, Winston. Good for you!"

She looked Erin in the eyes. "I have a favor to ask, Erin. In addition to a few dozen more cats, we're getting four horses. We could greatly use your help for another week. Do you think you can swing that?"

Erin leaned upon the porch railing. "I don't know, Maggie. My kids are getting ready for school and I really want to spend a few weeks with them before they go off for college. Being with them before they go is important to me."

Maggie nodded. "I understand. A few days maybe? At least until both sets of animals come in and we have them settled into their spaces? Since the lamb came a few weeks early, we're scrambling to make space for everyone, and now getting more horses, Mike will be attempting to create more places in the barn and section off another small pasture. Leslie can help him if you can cover the

Dog Palace and Kitty Castle for a few more days."

Erin saw the pleading in Maggie's eyes. She nodded and said, "Yes. I'll stay a few extra days. That will also give the cats and Winston more time to bond before we embark on the trip home."

Maggie smiled. "Thank you, Erin. I really appreciate this. We all do."

THAT EVENING before sunset, Mike secured wire to a wooden post a few feet from the barn. More fencing to his left helped create a new corral, the project he'd been working on all day. He didn't hear Erin walk up until she called out, "Hi, there, busy guy!"

He stopped his work and looked at her. Her large smile brought one to his face.

"Hi, yourself."

Mike noticed Winston beside her. He squatted down and said, "Hey there, fella. How are you and those cats doing?"

Winston, his tail wagging, sauntered up to Mike, and he patted the little dog's head.

"They've done very well," Erin responded as she walked closer. "A few hisses and growls by the cats at first, but with Winston's gentle, sweet personality, the Ricky and Rocket adjusted pretty quickly. Winston learned about cats while at Rhiann's sanctuary, so he knows not to push the limit. They all took about a thirty-minute nap on the couch before supper. I think Brittany's going to be quite happy with the boys."

As Mike drew to his full six-foot-one height, he noticed Erin held a cloth bag in her hand.

"You don't have the cats in there, do you?" he asked in a teasing voice as he pointed to the sack.

She laughed slightly and held up the bag. "I think you'd hear a lot of fussing. No, silly. I brought your supper. I've been hearing the pounding of nails all afternoon and saw you putting those posts in the ground earlier. I figured you could use a break."

She opened the container, which held two sandwiches, a small bag of potato chips, and a covered glass pitcher of lemonade. Her kindness startled him. Not that Erin wasn't thoughtful, but during her own busy day, settling in two cats, the thought that she would notice he hadn't taken a break in several hours touched his heart.

"Thank you, Erin. I appreciate your thoughtfulness," he said in a sincere voice.

She smiled and handed Mike the bag. He

reached for the lemonade first and poured a cup from the small thermos. After consuming the tart liquid, he said, "Ah! That hits the spot." He smiled. "I knew you were a good woman, Erin, I just didn't realize how much of an angel until now."

She blushed and smiled. "There are two ham and cheese sandwiches in there and a small bag of chips. Plus two peanut butter cookies for dessert."

Mike grinned. "I didn't know you had such food in your cabin. I know you're a salad and chicken girl."

"Maggie told me how much work you have ahead before the horses get here, so when I was in town earlier getting supplies for the cats and my extended stay, I picked up a bit extra."

"That's kind of you. What do you mean, your 'extended stay?'"

"Maggie asked me to stay on a bit, like you said she might. I agreed to a few extra days, with the cats and now horses coming in."

His eyes widened. "You did?"

She smiled and nodded. "I know you all can use another body for a bit longer. When I told Brittany and Brian this afternoon, they weren't too keen on the idea. But, when I explained the situation, they agreed I should stay a few more days. Besides, it gives Winston, Ricky, and Rocket more time to adjust to each other before our trip home."

Mike attempted to slow his happy, racing heart. He was sure Erin could hear the pounding. He took a deep breath and gave her a large smile.

"I'm glad you're staying. Yes, we can use the extra help the next few days. So, Maggie told you about the horses, did she?"

Erin nodded. "You're going to New Mexico to get them, she said."

This time Mike nodded. "I am. Not my favorite drive, Denver to Colorado Springs, but it's gotta be done."

"That's why the new corral?"

Again, Mike nodded. "With so much livestock right now, we need some extra space. Thankfully, the weather's still good, so we can move some animals outdoors for a few weeks."

"Well, I'd better let you get back to work. You'll lose light in another hour or so. And I need to finish Winston's evening walk and spend time with the cats."

"Thanks again, Erin, for the food."

She smiled. "Glad I could help out. Guess I'll see you tomorrow."

"Ah, Erin—would you mind if I stopped by

later, maybe bring some wine, and we can look at the stars together?"

The sweet smile stayed on her face.

"I'd enjoy that."

Mike's heart leaped, and he smiled. "I'll see you in a few hours then."

THAT NIGHT, with stars glimmering in the sky, Erin sat on one of the Adirondack chairs on the porch of her cabin; Mike sat on the second one. A table situated between them held a bottle of Chardonnay and Mike's wine glass. Erin held another glass in her hand, savoring the taste of the liquid she recently sipped.

"This is really good," she said, raising the glass toward Mike. "What's the brand?"

"It's called 15 Hands, out of Idaho."

"Crisp and fruity. Quite tasty," Erin responded and then she took another sip. "I didn't take you for a wine guy."

"Really? I enjoyed some of the best Washington wines while living in Seattle. Others, too, of course, but with so many vineyards in the state, that was something Elizabeth and I enjoyed – going to wineries and trying different varieties. I fashioned quite a palate for wine."

"Thanks for bringing the cheese and crackers as well," Erin said, as she nibbled a slice of Gouda, a light from the cabin's kitchen providing enough light for her to see the plate. "It's been awhile since supper."

Mike nodded. "I figured as much. Never drink on an empty stomach."

They grew quite as they listened to an owl hoot from the nearby forest. A group of coyotes chorused afterward. Erin smiled.

"Such an incredible night! Stars, owls, coyotes…no smog, car noises, bright lights. So peaceful."

She glanced at Mike, who was also staring into the dark.

"You really love it here, don't you?" Erin asked.

He looked over at her. She noticed a slight smile come to his face.

"I do," Mike responded in a low voice. "I'm thankful I found this place. It's a wonderful new chapter of my life."

"How did you adapt to the winters?"

He chuckled. "By taking time off." Surprise reflected on Erin's face and Mike laughed a bit more. "It's true. Maggie and I have an agreement—I generally take the month of January off. I spend time with my sons while they have a school break. I usually take several days off in the summer while they are here, and we go camping and fishing. But, in January, I not only spend time with them, but when they go back to college for the spring semester, I head south for a few weeks. New Mexico has become one of my favorite places. So has Arizona. I've gone to Mexico a few times for deep sea fishing as well. Then, when I come back, even though winter's still got a few months, I'm more rested and have gotten the sun and warmth I need."

"Huh," Erin said. "I guess I just thought you became like a mountain man or something."

Mike laughed and she grinned. "Believe me, February can be brutal here, but at least it's a short month."

Erin watched Mike reach for his wine glass and return his gaze to the darkened landscape. Suddenly, a *WHOOSH* came to her ears. She startled as a large, winged creature swooped near the porch.

"Gracious!"

Mike's hand covered her wrist, as she continued to hold her wine glass. "It's okay. Likely that owl we heard a bit ago. Out hunting for mice or rabbits, I'd guess."

"It's huge!"

He nodded. "Great-horned owls are decent-sized, especially close up. A person doesn't see one very often."

Erin noticed Mike's hand didn't leave her wrist. She realized she enjoyed the bond. She shifted the wine glass to her left hand and entwined her fingers through his. She glanced at him and discovered he was smiling at her. She gave him a quick smile and then fixed her gaze on the night sky.

"Very peaceful," she whispered. "Very nice."

She felt Mike's hand squeeze hers, and she relished the warmth, not only of their clasped hands, but of the shared companionship. As much as she tried to push away the feelings being near him produced, she had to admit to herself she was drawn to him. His compassionate demeaner, toward both animals and people, his toned and brawny physique, and his attention toward her added the spark that had gone out from her life after Daniel's diagnosis and death. That fire for life had slowly started to flicker again this year after spending time in Montana with Rhiann and Levi, helping them with their pet rescue and simply re-discovering herself amid the family history and majesty of Montana. Now, rekindling memories with Mike and getting to know him all over again, embers of thriving and not just simply surviving began to glimmer in her heart, mind, and soul. She sighed.

"Penny for your thoughts," Mike whispered.

She gave him a quick smile. "No real thoughts, just being in the moment. Something I started doing again fairly recently."

"A good place, I hope."

She nodded. "Yes, a good place."

She felt him squeeze her hand again, and she smiled before returning her gaze to the magical ink-colored sky.

"How about a horseback ride tomorrow evening?" she heard Mike ask. Erin looked at him. "I haven't had a chance yet to get you up to the higher pasture to see the Belgians." His eyes locked upon hers. "I promise to choose a gentle horse."

Erin smiled. "I think I'd like that.

The soft smile he gave her melted the reservations dancing within Erin's heart.

# Chapter 15

**THREE DAYS** later, Erin stood on the back porch of the Dog Palace. She watched six beagles that shared the space run and play while two others moseyed and sniffed. She awed once again at Maggie and Leslie's abilities to blend dogs together despite coming from different facilities and having different personalities. She thought about Jordan and Lauren's new addition and wondered how they were all doing on their trip. She made a mental note to call Lauren tonight. Perhaps she would make a trip back again in the fall after the kids were settled at school and visit Rhiann and Levi in Montana while in the area. She believed she was discovering a few more reasons to return.

Her thoughts tumbled around the previous day, spending most of the morning and into the afternoon with Mike. They traversed the Buffalo Bill Historical Center, spending hours visiting each exhibit hall. Mike's comments about and information on numerous displays educated Erin on western and natural history of the area and the art of people like Remington and Russell. She marveled at his knowledge and enthusiasm. American history had been a subject of interest for decades, and she absorbed the information he and the display panels provided. They shared lunch instead the small café within the museum's walls and finished touring the facility in early afternoon. Visiting the incredible historical center and listening to Mike whet her appetite about history once again, and she purchased several books and a few gifts for her children before they left the museum.

Mike had also taken her up the South Fork of the Shoshone River. The majestic scenery awed Erin, and the added thrill of seeing a herd of bighorn sheep for the first time delighted her. Mike also seemed to enjoy watching the creatures as he shared insights on the elusive animals.

He'd purchased dinner for them from a deli, and they shared the meal as well as more information about themselves on the porch of her cabin. They strolled with Winston to the barn and back, after checking on Hope and a new lamb born yesterday afternoon. Thankfully, no problems arose during this birth, and by the time Erin and Mike returned to Compassion Ranch late yesterday afternoon, Maggie, Kaitlyn, and Leslie had named the little male lamb Cody, after the nearby community.

Erin smiled at the memories. She knew she had found a circle of good friends, both of the human kind and of the animal variety. She also recognized how much she enjoyed Mike's company. She ran a finger across her lips, remembering the gentle press of his mouth upon hers before they parted company last night.

Erin's thoughts were interrupted by the rumbling of a truck. She walked to the fence and peered through the wire. She saw Maggie's pickup returning to the sanctuary.

"Here come the new cats, guys," she said to the dogs. "Time for me to get you in and settled for the rest of the afternoon."

She clapped her hands and commanded "Come!" Eight beagle faces looked at her. "Inside for treats!"

Thirty-two feet pounded the grass as the dogs bounded for the open back door and the two doggie doors on either side. Erin smiled.

"Works every time," she murmured as she turned and then walked inside the building.

ERIN WALKED into the barn. Maggie and Leslie hovered around twelve crates. Echoes of meows and whimpering came from within those carriers. Erin stopped and listened for a moment before continuing to walk to the two women.

"Hi, ladies."

They turned and smiled at her.

"We picked up our new residents without a hitch," Leslie said.

"I see that. Not happy campers, by the sounds they're making," Erin commented.

Leslie shrugged. "If you were a cat that had been on an airplane for three hours and then two more hours in a car, you probably wouldn't be happy either."

"You'll never guess who else hitched a ride with us from Billings," Maggie said, a sly grin on her face.

Erin looked at her. From around the corner of a horse stall stepped her daughter, Brittany. Erin's eyes widened as the young woman said with a smile, "Hey, Mom."

"Brittany!" Erin narrowed the gap between them in a few strides and embraced her twenty-four-year-old daughter. "What are you doing here?"

The young woman chuckled. "Good to see you, too, Mom."

"Oh, of course I'm delighted to see you." She pulled back and looked into her daughter's eyes. "This is such a surprise."

"That was the intention. You said Compassion Ranch needed your help so I thought you all might need mine as well. School isn't for another three weeks so I thought I'd come and help, and we could drive back together."

"You should be getting ready to go back to school. It's your last semester, and you need to focus."

"Mom, I'm not eighteen. I took the first few weeks of the month to get ready. I'm packed with what I need and all ready so that when we get back, we'll have a few more days together before I head out."

Erin's hands remained on Brittany's upper arms. "My firstborn—all grown and ready to take on the world."

"She called me last night and asked about coming to visit and staying with you," Maggie broke in. "I told her we'd be in Billings after noon today if she could get a flight that soon."

"Brit, that's a major expense, especially one-way."

"I have the majority of my rainy-day fund from Great-Grams so I took the money from that."

"That's really for you to help get settled after college," Erin reminded her daughter.

"I haven't touched the trust fund you and Dad set up. I told you that's my plan for it."

"I know, I know. I just don't want you to waste your Great-Grams' money on trips like this."

"It's a waste to come see my mother?"

"Ladies, I tell you what," Maggie interjected. "Leslie and I need to get these cats checked into our system and squared away for the night. Erin, why don't you get Brittany settled into the cabin and introduced to her new kitty companions? The two of you can meet us back here in about an hour. I'll get Kaitlyn, and we'll give names to these new cats."

"Sounds good to me!" Brittany said. She looked at Erin. "Mom? What do you say? I'm excited to meet the new furry friends you chose."

"Yes, of course. Winston will be happy to meet you, too."

"When Mike gets back tomorrow with the horses, he'll be checking over and vaccinating these guys," Maggie stated.

"Whose Mike?"

Maggie smiled. "I'll let your mother tell that story."

Brittany looked at Erin in surprise. "Mom?"

"He's the ranch manager and a veterinarian."

"Oh. Okay."

"I knew him in high school."

Brittany's eyes widened. "Oh, wow. That's a coincidence. Anything else I should know?"

Erin shook her head. "No, not right now."

"Later though?"

"Perhaps." Erin looked at Maggie. "We'll be back in about an hour."

"Take my truck. Brittany's bags are in it."

"Will do, thanks."

Erin and Brittany walked out of the barn and toward Maggie's pickup.

"I look forward to meeting the cats and Winston," Brittany said and then chuckled. "I can't believe Aunt Rhiann talked you into a dog."

"She didn't have to—Winston and I connected immediately."

"He must be a special dog."

"Oh, he is, my dear, he most certainly is!"

THAT EVENING, Brittany cuddled one of

her cats as she and her new feline friends sat on the couch. The second kitty batted a toy mouse between his paws. The brother swatted at Brittany's shoulder-length auburn hair.

"Well, that was fun," she commented as she pulled her hair back. "Naming and brushing the new cats. I like the wildflower names we came up with."

"Me, too," came Erin's reply as she continued stir-frying vegetables at the kitchen stove. She glanced at her daughter playing with the two cats. "Looks like you, Ricky, and Rocket are already good friends."

"They're going to be fun! They are already fun!" came Brittany's content reply. "Thanks for adopting them for me."

"We'll need to start taking them for rides in the car," Erin said. "It's a long way back to Florida."

"Yeah. After riding for two hours with twelve squalling cats, I'd rather not repeat that. I don't know how Maggie and Leslie do it."

"Love for the animals, knowing they're giving them a new chance at life. You do the same with dolphins and sea turtles."

"Yeah, but they don't make such a ruckus," Brittany replied. "But I get what you're saying."

Erin heard the couch squeak. She looked up and watched her daughter walk into the kitchen and lean against the counter.

"So, tell me about this Mike guy."

Erin tried not to blush, but she felt certain Brittany saw the crimson dawn on her cheek for her eyebrows arched and her voice rose a bit when she said, "You feel something for him!"

"Brit, it's not what you think."

"What is it then?"

"Complicated." Erin sighed, turned off the stove, and walked to the dining table. Brittany followed. After each claimed a chair, Erin looked into her daughter's eyes and said, "It's a long story."

"I'm not going anywhere."

Erin sighed, looked away for a moment, and then returned her gaze to Brittany's face. In a quiet voice, Erin said, "You know Aunt Rhiann and I lost our parents when we were teenagers and that we moved from Idaho to Washington to live with our Grams and Grandpop." Brittany nodded. "I was a senior in high school and barely knew anyone, even by January. Mike Jacobs was in my algebra class. He was a whiz at science and math, and he became my tutor, helping me get caught up. We became friends. He was kind at a time I needed a friend. He took me to prom, and though we had feelings for each other, I was returning to Boise where Rhiann and I grew up to attend college, and he was going to Seattle to become a veterinarian. We never saw each other after that."

"Never?"

Erin shook her head. "Until I arrived here. I had no idea he was the ranch manager. Upon talking a bit, we came to realize who each other was."

"So, how's that been, meeting up with him again after all these years?"

Erin bit her lower lip. "Interesting. Mike has admitted he has feelings for me, that he always had."

"Oh, Mom..."

Erin held up a hand. "I'm a recent widow, and he knows that. Mike also lost his spouse, but longer ago than we lost your dad. I'm not...I'm not ready for another relationship right now, and Mike knows that. His kindness and compassion are still a big part of who he is ..."

"Being a veterinarian and working here, I can see that," Brittany said in a low voice.

Erin nodded. "He's giving me all the time I need to grieve. He understands what grief is. He and his wife had two sons, and so in addition to working here, they are his focus, just like you and Brian are mine."

Brittany reached across the table and clasped her mother's hands. "Mom, Brian and I are nearly on our own. We want you to be happy; Dad wanted you to be happy. So, if this Mike guy does that, you shouldn't turn your back on him."

"I'm not. We are taking it slow. I'm very flattered Mike…feels something for me. Your dad and I had a wonderful relationship, a loving, solid marriage. Nearly twenty-eight years of my life was spent with him. I still need time to adjust to him not being there."

Brittany nodded. "I know. After being at the house for about six weeks, I kept having to remind myself he's not there."

Erin squeezed her daughter's hand. "I've been thinking that when Brian is done with school in the next few years, I should downsize. You'll be off on your own by then and he'll be starting his career. I don't need such a big house when the two of you are making your way in the world."

"Mom, that's our family home!"

Erin nodded. "I know. But we've lived in many houses, and that's just what they are: houses. Family makes a home, and that's wherever we are together. Look at your Aunt Rhiann—she lived with our Grams and Grandpop in two different places in Washington and now she's made a home in Montana."

"Aunt Rhiann never had kids, never raised them in a house. She's been a free-spirit all of her life," Brittany retorted.

Erin looked deeply into her daughter's brown eyes. "Brit, your Aunt Rhiann gave up many things she loved, including her former fiancé,' to care for our grandparents. She's now making a home with Levi and continues doing what she loves, what she's passionate about, and making a difference. Where a person lives isn't important; making a home and making a difference is."

"What are you passionate about, Mom? What do you love?"

"Besides you and your brother and my sister?" She shrugged. "I'm still figuring that out."

Silence passed between them for a moment. Brittany sighed and said, "If you decide to sell the house, I'll support your decision. It is a big place, and Daddy took very good care of us. You're right— we all must find our way, and Brian and I shouldn't stand in yours. I think you've found a passion here, Mom. Perhaps this is where you belong."

Erin laughed. "Oh, I don't know about that. I may have been raised in Idaho and eastern Washington, but I'm not a woman who likes western winters. Besides, I don't want to be that far away from you and Brian."

"We don't know where we'll be. Even if we stay in Florida the first part of our careers, no one knows if that's where we'll be in ten years."

Erin nodded. "That's true, but I can't see either of you enduring harsh winters either."

Brittany smiled. "We are pretty spoiled."

Erin squeezed her daughter's hands again. "We'll just take it a step at a time. You still have this semester and Brian still has two more years. No big decisions, like selling the house, need to be made now. We're still grieving, all of us, and we need the time to continue going through that process."

She stood up. "Let me finish cooking dinner and then we'll take Winston for a walk. I want you to meet a couple of special sheep."

# Chapter 16

**MIKE DROVE** his truck with a six-stall horse trailer attached down the Compassion Ranch drive and pulled up next to the barn. During the trip to and from New Mexico, he thought about Erin. Maggie had texted him earlier today to let him know Erin's daughter arrived. Although he tried to calm his nerves by focusing on the horses, anxiety clouded his brain and heart. He stopped the truck and pulled the emergency brake. Traveling nearly two days with nervous horses also kept his mind occupied. Relief coursed through his body as the familiar buildings and landscape surrounded him.

Maggie walked out of the barn and greeted him with a smile.

"Welcome back."

"Thanks. It's good to be back. These guys are a handful, I'll warn you. It will take two of us to handle one horse."

"Well, you'll be glad to know all the sheep and lambs are doing well. We had another birth earlier today and nothing went awry. Hope and the other lamb have had a few meetings and that's gone well. Once that one is old enough, I'm sure they'll be fast friends."

"Did you come up with a name?"

Maggie smiled. "I thought you did."

"Well, just because I like 'Miracle' doesn't mean that's what her name should be."

"You helped her and her mother, so yes, I think you should name her. Miracle is just fine – and pretty appropriate."

Mike smiled. "Okay, Miracle it is. So, how are the new cats? You said you got them back here safely and in a timely fashion."

Maggie nodded. "Still confined and waiting for you. Leslie, Erin, and Brittany worked at the Kitty Castle all morning cleaning and preparing the intake section for them."

"How are Erin and her daughter?"

"As far as I can tell, good. There was a bit of spitting and hissing, like with those new cats, at the start, but I think they've worked things out."

"And now I show up."

"Perhaps speak to Erin before meeting Brittany. The boat's already been rocked a bit."

"Good idea. Well, let's take care of the cats

first and let these horses settle a bit before removing them from the trailer." They began walking toward the barn. "What about the family we're expecting?"

"On track for coming in tomorrow afternoon as far as I know."

"Good. My nephew is driving in tomorrow, too. He's on his way back to Washington for his senior year of college, and I told him about the horses. He's a great hand, having worked two summers at a dude ranch near Laramie. He can stay a couple of days before having to be at Washington State in Pullman."

"Excellent! I was hoping we'd see Jason again this summer."

Mike nodded. "Me, too, and just in time. I'm going to need an extra hand these next few days with this equine group."

AN HOUR later, as he sat on a bale of hay inside the barn, Mike called Erin's cell phone. After she picked up and said hello, he smiled and stated, "Hi, Erin, it's Mike. How are you doing?"

"Fine," she replied. "How was your trip?"

"Good. A bit of a challenge through Colorado, but that's nothing new. I hear you have a surprise visitor."

"I do."

He heard the cautious tone of her voice. "Everything okay?"

"Yes, as far as I know."

"Have you mentioned me?"

"Yes. Somewhat."

"I just wanted to find out where I stand. Proceed with caution, I take it."

"Yes, I would. Are the horses okay?"

"They are. Maggie and I will be getting them out of the trailer in the next hour. If you and Brittany would like, stop down after supper. They're a lovely group but they're going to need a lot of work. You can at least see them when we get them into that new corral I built."

"I think we'd like that."

"The cats are ready to go up to the Kitty Castle if you two want to help Leslie first."

"Sounds good. Let her know we'll be there in about forty minutes."

"I'll do that. See you later."

"Okay, bye."

She clicked off before he did. Mike bit his lip as he hung up.

"How'd it go?" asked Maggie.

"She sounded tense."

Maggie nodded. "Understandable. Give them time, Mike, and a bit of space."

He nodded. "I plan to."

ERIN FELT Brittany's eyes on her. The younger woman sat on the couch with Winston in her lap and one cat sleeping above her shoulders across the top of the couch. The other tabby lay sprawled next to Brittany.

"Who was that?"

"Mike. He's back with the horses and invited us down to see the animals. First, though, we can help Leslie settle the new cats into the Kitty Castle if you want."

Brittany smiled. "I'd like that. When? Now?"

Erin shook her head. "After dinner. Are you good with grilled chicken on salad? I have some chicken left over from the other night."

"Sure. That was a big lunch Maggie fed us. She's a nice woman."

Erin nodded. "That she is."

She walked to the refrigerator and began pulling items from the appliance to create the meal. "I'll just warm up this chicken if you want to cut tomatoes and mushrooms for our salad."

She heard Brittany rise from the couch. Winston gave a whoof of disapproval and when she looked over, Erin saw him turn a few times before settling on the spot her daughter had vacated. Neither cat seemed disturbed and continued napping. As Erin drew a cutting board from the counter next to the refrigerator, Brittany walked into the kitchen. She ran water at the sink and washed her hands.

"I wonder where they're going to keep these new horses?" Brittany pondered. "There's not much room in that barn with the sheep, including Miracle and Hope, and the four horses already stabled."

"Mike built a new enclosure next to the barn. I believe he intends to erect a large shed for a temporary shelter."

"They should try for a grant. You could help them with that."

"Maggie and Kaitlyn are already working on one, as I understand things," Erin responded.

She placed some chicken into a pan and turned on the heat to warm the meat. Brittany began chopping lettuce, tomatoes, and mushrooms. Erin peeled a small avocado and started to slice it.

"You know, Mom. Dad asked you to set up that foundation. Perhaps we should consider helping Compassion Ranch with some of those funds."

Erin looked at her daughter. "Your dad wanted scholarships created with that."

Brittany nodded. "Why can't we do both? He helped Aunt Rhiann a few years ago."

Erin mulled her daughter's words. "I like that idea, helping both groups."

Brittany looked at her. "I think Dad would have liked that, too." She grinned. "He even helped the sea turtle organization where I interned, if you remember. I'm sure he'd want to help here."

Erin kissed her daughter's cheek and smiled. "I think you're right, and yes, I do remember. He was proud of you then, and I know he'd be proud of you now."

"He'd be proud of you, too, Mom."

The two women looked at each other, and Erin wrapped her arms around her daughter.

# Chapter 17

**AN HOUR** later, Erin and Brittany helped Leslie secure the door to the quarantine area of the Kitty Castle. The three women looked through the large glass window as twelve cats explored the room. Toys littered the floor and two tall cat trees butted against two large windows. Another climbing post extended toward the window the women looked through, and a carpeted perch attached to the sill. An orange and white longhaired cat jumped onto the soft roost, startling the three women.

"Oh!" exclaimed Brittany, stepping back.

"She must have wondered where we disappeared to," Leslie said with a slight laugh.

"Think they'll settle in all right?"

"Yes," Leslie responded to Brittany's question. "There's always scrapes between cats at first, but these lads and lasses seem like overall good cats. They'll work out their differences and the pecking order. I'll check on them later tonight."

"Well, I guess we have horses to see," Erin said with a slight smile.

"Not to mention a certain cowboy," Leslie said, grinning.

Erin and Brittany looked at her. From behind her daughter, Erin gave a frown and a shake of her head. Leslie caught on.

"I mean, we need to welcome Mike back. Traveling through Colorado Springs and Denver with a loaded horse trailer can be a dangerous trek."

She turned on her heel and headed for the door. Brittany looked at her mother, who simply shrugged. "Let's go see the horses. I need to walk Winston soon, too."

She and Brittany followed Leslie outside of the Kitty Castle and together, the three women walked to the barn. Erin heard neighs and whinnies before reaching the structure where the livestock lived. A large yard light helped guide them toward the barn and attached corral, which confined six varied horses: two bays, one brown with a black mane and tail, one red appaloosa, two paints, one brown and white and the other brown, black and white. Erin's eyes locked on that mare, its two-toned mane flowing in the breeze. Sturdy legs and strength of build brought out the sense of powerful character in the animal.

"What a beautiful horse!" she breathed aloud.

"Which one, Mom? I think they're all gorgeous!" Brittany said in a low voice.

"I agree with Brittany," Leslie said. "These are among the most magnificent horses we've had."

"The paint, the one with all three colors and black and white mane."

"Oh, yeah. It is lovely. I like the appy as well. Reminds me of the horse Uncle Levi had last spring. There's some gorgeous horses in his herd."

Erin nodded. "Levi and Rhiann would love these horses."

Leslie looked at the two women. "Think they'd be interested in adopting?"

"Perhaps. I don't know," Erin said.

Brittany looked at her. "We should ask them. Maybe they'd at least come and look at them."

"You may be right, Brit."

The ladies continued their walk. Erin noticed Maggie standing at the fence and focused strolling toward her. Maggie smiled at the trio as they arrived.

"Gorgeous animals, aren't they?"

"They sure are!" Leslie said. "I bet Mike's enthralled with them."

"Is he a horse guy?" Brittany asked.

"Mike's an animal guy, period," Leslie said. "He's a vet. In fact, he saved one of our sheep the other night who had a difficult birth."

"Your mom helped us," Maggie chimed in.

"She did?" Brittany looked at Erin, who shrugged.

"I didn't do much."

"Don't let her fool you," came Mike's deep voice as he rounded the corner from the barn. He smiled at the women. "All of these ladies did fine work. Without their help, our ewe and her lamb might have died."

Mike tipped his brown Stetson and held out his arm. "I'm Mike Jacobs, ranch manager and sanctuary veterinarian. I presume you're Brittany Christensen."

"I am indeed," Brittany said as she shook Mike's hand. "Nice to meet you, Dr. Jacobs."

"Oh, no formalities here, young lady. We all do our part at this sanctuary and we're all equal."

She smiled. "Mike it is then."

Erin saw Mike's quick smile to her before he turned to gaze at the horses. "Nice-looking group, aren't they?"

"Sure are," Leslie said. "Glad you and the horses made it back safely, Mike."

"Thanks. Me, too. That stretch between Denver and Colorado Springs seems to get worse every year."

"Try Orlando to Miami," Brittany interjected. "I'm glad I'm about done with school and hope work takes me out of that rat-race."

Erin looked at her daughter in surprise. "I thought you loved the area."

"The ocean and beauty, yeah. The traffic and population ..." She shook her head. "No."

"Well, there's plenty of ocean around the country. I'm sure you'll find your happy place," Mike commented.

"I take it you've found yours here at Compassion Ranch?" Brittany inquired.

He looked at her. "That I have. Although I enjoyed Seattle, too. It was a great place for a career."

"Mm, I may have to look into it," Brittany pondered.

"If you're used to Florida sunshine, Seattle likely isn't your best spot," Mike said.

At that moment, the paint horse Erin spied earlier broke from the group and sauntered over to the people at the fence.

"What's their story, Mike?" Erin asked as she watched the horse approach.

"Nutrition studies," he said.

"What does that mean?" Brittany asked.

"The animals are used by food companies to test different types of products. These horses, for example, lived most of their lives at an agricultural test site and were given a variety of new feed during the past ten-plus years."

"Just like the cats we brought in," Leslie commented.

"Animals are used in a lot of research projects," Mike said. "We're here for them when those studies are completed. That's our purpose."

"Such animals didn't have a place to go before Compassion Ranch," added Maggie.

"I remember you telling me that the other day," said Brittany. "Now I more fully understand your mission."

"It's a great mission," Mike said. "Without Compassion Ranch, all the animals now at the sanctuary would have been euthanized."

After a moment of silence, Erin said, "Brittany and I have some news for you all. We want to donate some funds toward the new barn that's needed." She felt everyone's eyes on her face and glanced from person to person. "Daniel left funds for a foundation. We want to use some of that money to help Compassion Ranch."

"Erin, that's so wonderful! Thank you!" Maggie said in a shocked voice.

Erin smiled. "Let's get together tomorrow and work out the details."

Brittany looped her arm through her mother's with a smile.

"Dad would have wanted to be part of this," she said.

Erin smiled at her daughter and at her new friends. "Yes, he would, so in his honor and memory, we will contribute to this great mission."

She glanced at Mike to find him watching her. She felt a soft nudge to her cheek and turned slightly. She heard a couple of intakes of breath as her eyes met the soft brown ones of the tri-colored paint horse. Erin also inhaled as the mare again nuzzled her face.

"Oh, Mom!" whispered Brittany.

A tear formed in Erin's left eye. She blinked and then slowly extended her hand toward the horse, letting her smell and rub. She scratched the mare's chin and caressed her soft nose. The animal leaned her face into Erin's. Tears gathered in Erin's eyes and trickled down her cheek. She felt Mike's breath and listened as he whispered into her ear, "She's chosen you. She's the horse I was most concerned about and now look at her. She needs you, and she knows you need her. Horses are smart that way."

"She's amazing," Erin whispered.

"So are you," Mike whispered back.

Erin glanced at him, and their eyes locked for a moment. Mike gave her a gentle smile. Erin turned away to again rub the side of the paint's nose. She caught Brittany staring at her. Erin gave her daughter a shy smile before returning her attention to the mare.

"You are a beauty, girl," she said in a low tone. "I hope we'll be friends."

MIKE HEARD Erin whisper to the horse. He glanced away as moisture glistened in his eyes. He knew the connection people and animals formed – he'd experienced it, and witnessed it, many times. He knew without a doubt at that moment he loved Erin. Would his heart again break because of that love? He decided right then he would risk everything, including heartbreak, to be with her.

# Chapter 18

**THE NEXT** morning as Erin brushed her hair in the bathroom, she heard Brittany talking in a low, but audible tone.

"You should see her, Brian. The horse is gorgeous, and she and Mom bonded immediately." Her voice paused. "Well, I don't know. Maybe it will go live at Aunt Rhiann's sanctuary." Another pause. "Yes, Mom is fine, and she loves it here, I can tell." Again, a pause. "Well, I don't know. Whatever she wants to do."

Erin smiled as she finished brushing her hair. She heard the exasperation in Brittany's voice and could just imagine what her twenty-two-year-old son was thinking and saying to his sister. She started to step out of the bathroom when Brittany's voice lowered even more.

"This guy named Mike, the veterinarian – he and Mom knew each other in high school, and I know he's looking for Mom to replace the wife he lost. Just the way he looks at her…I felt weird."

Erin stopped in the small hallway. She listened as Brittany continued, "Dad hasn't been gone two years yet, but I don't know…This guy is compassionate, a professional, and he genuinely seems to love Mom. Although it's a bit weird, I think he would treat her as sweet as Dad did."

Erin deduced Brian was speaking as Brittany remained quiet for a few moments before saying, "I'm not sure how Mom feels—I think she's still figuring that out. But, little brother, I wouldn't be surprised if she and Mike spent more time together before we leave." Another pause. "Yes, of course, I'm okay with it. Mom is still young, and you know Dad told her not to mourn him forever. She deserves to be loved. We're not going to always be there with her. I don't want her to be lonely and unhappy."

Erin smiled and shook her head. She raised her face to the ceiling and whispered, "We raised two great kids, Daniel. Thank you for the blessing of them...and of you."

MIKE SPENT time with the new horses in the corral he'd constructed. He groomed each animal with the livestock brush and currycomb. He spoke in a calm tone, helping them accustom themselves to his voice and hand. Although the animals were not skittish, neither were they exceedingly happy with his presence. He still marveled at the tri-colored paint's reaction to Erin last night. He and Cisco shared the same bond and established that at first meeting, so he knew what he was talking about when he whispered to Erin last night.

He startled when he heard her voice from the gate. "How's that horse of mine?"

Mike turned around to find her smiling. He returned the facial expression.

"Come find out for yourself."

He watched her open the gate, walk into the corral, and then close the access. At that moment, the horse they talked about broke from the group and trotted to her new human friend. Erin, just inside the enclosure, stood still. The mare slowed her pace and walked to her. She again pressed her cheek to Erin's face. Mike observed the woman stroke the horse's chin and then behind her ears. Erin then ran her hand down the mare's neck. The horse shuddered, not in fear but with gladness, and nuzzled Erin's neck. She wrapped her arms around the creature. Mike heard Erin's soft cries. He turned back to the other horses and let Erin and the paint have their moment. He knew the therapy that animals provided, and the way the horse had sensed Erin's need for comfort caused him to choke up. He concentrated brushing the appaloosa's shoulders and didn't hear Erin walk up behind him. However, he felt her gentle touch upon his shoulder.

"Thank you," she whispered. He turned. She stepped back, likely started to see the mist in his eyes. "I'm sorry. I didn't mean…"

He smiled and shook his head. "Nothing to be sorry for." He slipped a hand into hers while the currycomb remained in his other hand. "I know how connected one can get to an animal. I've seen it, I've experienced it. Dogs, horses, cats, even rabbits. People and animals bond, there is no doubt."

He kissed the top of Erin's hand. "I'm glad for you…and for her." Mike nodded at the paint who stood just behind Erin.

"Winston and I had the same connection when he came into Rhiann's rescue," Erin said in a low voice. She wrapped an arm around the horse's neck as her hand remained tucked into Mike's. "There was no doubt I'd take him to Florida with me, but what am I going to do with a horse? She's not even trained to ride, and I don't have a place to keep her down there."

Mike smiled. "She can stay here. I'll work with her, train her, and when you come back for a visit, she'll be all ready for you to ride."

Erin looked at him. "I haven't said I was coming back."

His smile didn't fade. "Perhaps you have a reason to…or maybe a couple of reasons to."

She returned his smile. "Perhaps."

Mike's gaze left her face and focused on a

nearby hillside. In a low voice, he said, "Remember me telling you about Hank?" He glanced at her and Erin nodded. Mike returned his gaze to the hill "He's buried on that bluff near the tree line."

He sensed Erin move closer. "Hank was for me what this horse is for you, and Cisco is for me what Winston is for you. They're all healers in their own unique way."

Erin's arm encircled his waist. He glanced at her and, after a short gaze, she lay her head on his shoulder. They stood in silence under the azure Wyoming sky even after the mare placed her chin atop the Erin's right shoulder.

A FEW hours later, Erin sat behind a computer in the administrative office. Kaitlyn stood near a file cabinet placing invoices into folders while Maggie and Leslie talked in low tones in Maggie's office. Despite the whispering, Erin caught words and phrases pertaining to the new volunteers coming to help later in the day, discussing who would be assigned to what project area.

Erin heard Maggie say, "Mike's nephew will be working with the horses, so you can place the

Brown family members with the cats, including our 'flower children,' as well as at the Dog Palace, and maybe with the sheep and cows, depending on what Brittany wants to do."

Erin heard wheels roll and looked up to see Leslie, the chair she sat in close to the doorway, peek around the door and ask, "What do you think, Erin? Is Brittany tired of the livestock?"

"I can't speak for my daughter. You'll need to ask her."

"I tried calling earlier but she didn't pick up. I left her with cats this morning but haven't seen her since," said Leslie.

"Maybe she went back to the cabin to check on Winston, Ricky, and Rocket." Her eyes caught something on the computer screen. "I found it!"

"What?" Leslie asked.

A large grin came upon Erin's face. "The grant I told Maggie about. My sister received a grant from the PetSmart Foundation last year. I just couldn't remember the timing, but here it is." Her voice resounded with glee. "There's still time to apply!"

Leslie scrambled from her chair, and she and Maggie jogged into the main office. Kaitlyn left her filing station to join them. All three women gathered around Erin and peered at the screen.

"The deadline is 5 pm tomorrow," Erin announced.

"Oh, there's no way to meet that," Kaitlyn lamented.

Erin looked up. "Really? It's only two o'clock. We have more than twenty-four hours."

"Yeah, but, that's not enough time. We can't possibly compile all the necessary information and care for the animals and greet the new volunteers, and ...."

"Kaitlyn, we are four capable women. We can split up duties and get it done," Maggie said in a firm tone. She then looked at Erin. "Tell us what to do."

"First, gather the paperwork from your most successful grant of the past two years. We can work off that and update what we need. Second, gather your most recent financials, and third, decide what project is most necessary."

"That's easy—the barn," Leslie said.

"And we can use your commitment as matching funds," Maggie said.

Erin looked at Kaitlyn. "What do you say, Kaitlyn? In this with us?"

The young woman grinned. "Let's do this!"

AT 6 pm, Erin tapped the piles of papers together as Kaitlyn locked the file cabinets located along the wall shared with Maggie's office.

"Everything is here. Tomorrow we'll scan these and put them into a zip file with the written documentation and photos. I still need to edit some of Maggie's proposal, but we're well on our to get this grant application out tomorrow," Erin said.

Kaitlyn walked to her desk and slipped the file cabinet key into the top drawer. "I didn't mean to sound like a nay-sayer earlier. I was just concerned about us getting our hopes up and reaching for a straw that might break. It happens now and then when deadlines creep up."

Erin looked at her. "I have to admit, Kaitlyn, I've wondered a bit about your feelings of me being here. The first time we met and even earlier today, I've felt you didn't want me here."

The younger woman looked at her, sighed, and pulled out her desk chair. After seating herself, she looked at Erin and said, "I guess I've been jealous... and worried. You have so much experience writing grants and dealing with businesses and organizations. I've been afraid of losing my job, especially when I heard how much non-profit grant writing experience you've had the past five years."

Erin stared at her. "Kaitlyn, I'm not here to take your job. I'm a volunteer, and I'm going back home soon. I'm here simply to help wherever and however I can. Maggie hired you for your bookkeeping and other skills. You both have been learning more about grants and you've been successful. I'm just piggybacking off what you both have already done these last few years."

"We weren't always successful."

"No organization is. You just keep trying, and that's what the two of you have done."

"It's not easy juggling grant writing, bookkeeping, visitor stays, volunteer placements, animal intakes, membership registrations, fundraising events, and the numerous other things I have to do."

Erin nodded. "I'd think not. A lot is required of the small staff here."

"That's for sure. It's just … I get nervous sometimes about not being good enough, and with a wedding next year…"

Erin's eyes widened. "A wedding?"

Kaitlyn smiled. "My boyfriend proposed on my birthday in May, and we're planning a wedding for next June."

"Congratulations!"

"Thanks. I just can't lose my job. We want to take a honeymoon cruise to the Bahamas, and between the cost of the wedding and the honeymoon, we're saving every nickel we can."

"I understand. Please don't worry—I'm not taking your job. I'm sorry you thought that."

"I'm sorry for being suspicious and rude."

"You weren't rude. Cool, perhaps."

"Either way, I'm sorry."

Erin smiled. "All is forgiven." She stood. "I'll set these on Maggie's desk in case she wants to review them before she goes home this evening. I'll see you in the morning, and we can get all this squared away to send off."

"Have a good night, Erin."

"You, too, Kate. Thanks for all your help."

The young woman smiled and nodded. "Thanks so much for yours. I can envision that new barn already!"

Erin returned her smile. "Me, too."

After placing the paperwork onto Maggie's desk, Erin walked toward the external office door.

Brittany burst through the door. Erin stepped back.

"Oh, Brit! You nearly ran me over."

Grinning, her daughter responded, "Sorry, Mom. I just had to tell you—Mike got a halter on the paint! He wants you to come and see."

Erin returned her daughter's smile. "By all means. Let's have a look." She glanced back at Kaitlyn. "Wanna come?"

The younger woman smiled and shook her head. "You go on. I'll stop by before I leave for the evening."

Erin closed the door and turned to her daughter. "Lead the way."

Still smiling, Brittany said, "He's really great with the horses, all the animals actually. You should have seen him working with them this afternoon!"

Maggie met the two women on the steps. "I hear the paint is doing exceptionally well. I just ate a quick dinner and was heading to the barn to check on the residents. I assume you're heading that way— mind if I tag along?"

"No, that would be great," Erin said. "I put the grant materials in your inbox so you can review them tonight or first thing tomorrow."

"Excellent, thanks, Erin."

A Chevy pickup ambled up the gravel road. The women watched as the vehicle stopped near the office building. "Jason's here," Maggie commented.

"Whose Jason?" Brittany asked.

"Mike's nephew. He's stopping on his way back to Washington to help Mike with the horses for a few days."

The window of the pickup rolled down and a man about twenty-five with jet black hair and a moustache and trimmed beard stuck his head out the window. His tanned face displayed a deep, sincere smile. Erin heard her daughter's breath catch. She glanced at Brittany and caught her staring at the handsome man.

"Hey, there, Maggie!" he said. "I hear you can use an extra ranch hand for a few days."

"Need for you to put those wrangling skills to work, Jason, so yes! Glad you're here," the sanctuary director stated. She looked at Erin and Brittany. "Jason Fletcher, I'd like you to meet Mrs. Erin Christiansen and her daughter Brittany. They're volunteering with us for a few more days."

Jason saluted them with two fingers to his forehead. "Ladies. Nice to meet you. I hope you're enjoying your stay at Compassion Ranch as much as I do when I'm able."

"I understand you brought something for

your uncle," Maggie said with a grin on her face.

The young man smiled back. "Well, yeah, if he wants her, that is."

"Oh, I imagine he'll be excited to see her. He's already talked about her a few times," Maggie said. Erin looked at the director with a slight frown. "He's at the barn, which is where we're headed."

"I'll see you ladies down there then."

"I have an open cabin if you want it," Maggie told Jason before he could put the truck into DRIVE.

"I'll bunk with Mike if he's okay with it," Jason responded. "I don't want to dirty up another place for just a few days. See you ladies in a bit!"

Jason acknowledged them with a grin and a nod. He then coasted the vehicle toward the barn. Erin watched, an unsettled feeling in her stomach. *Who is this 'she' Maggie and Jason talked about? I didn't see anyone in the truck with him.*

"Nice kid," Maggie commented. "I always enjoy having him here, even if only for a few days."

Erin continued watching Jason's truck as it came to a stop near the corral. After the young man angled himself from the vehicle, he turned back toward the front of the truck. To her surprise, a black and tan dog leaped from the interior, landing with ease on the ground.

"Oh!" Erin exclaimed.

Maggie and Brittany turned to look at her.

"What, Mom?" her daughter asked.

"A dog!"

Maggie chuckled as she and Brittany watched the medium-haired canine follow Jason into the barn.

"That's Mike's new four-footed companion. Hopefully anyway."

"Is that the 'she' you and Jason mentioned?" Erin inquired.

Smile still on her face, Maggie nodded. "Sure is. Mike told me the other day that Jason planned to bring a dog for him to check out. If Mike wants her, he can keep her. Otherwise, Jason will take the dog to his parents."

"Why doesn't Jason keep it?" Brittany asked.

Maggie began walking toward the barn; Brittany and Erin fell in step beside her.

"He's finishing college—no time for a dog right now," Maggie responded.

"How did he come to have it in the first place?" asked Brittany.

"Jason's worked at a dude ranch down by

Laramie the past two summers. One day earlier this year, the dog just showed up, skinny and worn out. Jason and the owners deduced someone either lost the dog in the woods or dumped her. They tried finding the owners for rest of the summer but had no luck. The ranch closes in a few weeks and the owners really couldn't keep her, so Jason spoke to Mike about her. I'm hoping he'll take her. He hasn't chosen another dog since Hank died."

"Hank?" Brittany inquired.

"I'll tell you later, sweetheart. Mike shared the story with me this morning," Erin said.

"Anyway, Jason interned with the Washington Game and Fish a few years ago," Maggie said. "Mike says he's gotten another internship with them again next spring, and he finishes his classes in wildlife biology this fall."

"Umm," Brittany murmured. "Sounds like we have a few things in common."

Erin looked at her daughter. *I think this young man has caught my girl's attention.*

# Chapter 19

**"THANK YOU** for inviting us to dinner," Erin said.

She and Brittany sat next to each other in a booth at Sadie Mae's, the restaurant where she had dined with Mike earlier in the week. Mike and his nephew sat across from them.

"Yes, this is quite nice," Brittany affirmed.

"Well, our last meal was interrupted by a sheep in labor, and with Jason just arriving this evening, I thought a meal out would be in order," Mike said.

"Everything turned out okay with the ewe, I take it," Jason said.

"Yes, thanks to help from the women at Compassion Ranch," Mike responded.

Brittany shook her head. "I can't believe my mother helped deliver a lamb."

Erin looked at her. "Why ever not? I delivered you and your brother, didn't I?"

Brittany blushed and dropped her head.

"She gotcha there, Brittany," Jason said in a teasing voice.

The young woman looked up, and Erin noticed her daughter was captivated by the tease, the smile, and the man's dancing hazel eyes. She caught Mike looking at her; the two older people shared a secret smile.

"So, about your new dog…" Erin prompted.

Mike grinned. "She's great!"

"I told you she was, but oh, no, you didn't believe me," Jason said with a grin.

Mike shrugged. "A man's gotta meet the creature for himself."

"So does a woman," Erin said.

Mike smiled. "You're right."

"So, you're going to keep her, I take it?" Brittany asked.

"And you're right, too," Mike responded with a smile and a twinkle in his eyes.

"What's her name?" Erin asked.

"At the ranch, we called her Shadow," Jason said. "She always followed people around."

"She'll continue to have that name," said Mike. "No sense trying to make her learn another name. She's used to Shadow, it seems."

Jason nodded. "She is. She's responded well to training."

"Which I'll keep up. If she's going to hang out with me at the sanctuary, I need to be comfortable with her knowledge of obedience commands."

"You said she's a German shepherd mix?" Erin asked.

Mike nodded. "Possibly mixed with Airedale—that type of terrier has similar ears and are generally brown and white. Shepherds of course can be any color, including black and brown. Both breeds are quite intelligent."

Jason nodded. "And we found out she's that, right quick!"

Brittany shook her head. "I can't believe anyone would dump a dog. That's plain cruel."

"I'm afraid it happens all the time, whether in the city or in rural areas," Jason commented.

A moment of silence passed before Brittany spoke again. "Well, thanks for rescuing her, Jason." He smiled. "I hear you're studying wildlife biology."

The young man nodded. "That I am. Thinking of going into wildlife veterinary science."

"Wow, that's cool! I'm finishing my degree in marine biology."

The young man's eyes lit up. "No kidding! Awesome. Have you done an internship yet?"

"Three," she responded. "Two with Sea World and one with Sea Turtle Rescue of the Keys."

"Impressive. I've done only one so far, but I have another scheduled next spring. I finish classes in December and start interning with Washington Game and Fish next February. I'll likely continue through the fall and perhaps begin wildlife vet school the next January. Or I may work a year or two and go back later."

"It's always a tough decision what to do after course work's completed," Brittany acknowledged.

"So, what's been your favorite animal to work with thus far?" Jason asked.

"Dolphins. They are so intelligent and gentle! Too many of them are dying from red tide and other foul stuff. We need to get a handle on ocean pollution, including lost fishing nets and plastics to keep marine life populations thriving."

He nodded. "I agree."

"What about you? What animals do you enjoy working with?"

"Big cats. Mountain lion and lynx primarily."

"Oh, yeah. I can see where they'd be fascinating. You know, Mom and I adopted two tabby cats from Compassion Ranch, and as I've been getting to know them, I'm more and more in awe of their abilities and intelligence."

Jason nodded enthusiastically. "Have you ever seen a wild cat? The way they stalk, the way they move through the forest, their hunting skills...just everything about them is incredible."

The waitress brought their meals. Jason grinned and said, as he picked up his fork, "Conversation to be continued."

Erin saw Brittany's beautiful smile and her nod of agreement. Again, she glanced at Mike, who raised his eyebrows and smiled.

LATER, ON the porch of the cabin, Jason said to Brittany, "Your mother chose cool cats."

"Aren't they neat? They settled into the cabin so well, she said, and they're doing great on car rides, too. They'll settle in well with us in Florida, I'm sure."

"We're going to let you two talk some more

and take Winston for a walk," Mike declared.

He took the dog's leash from inside the cabin door and led Erin and the spaniel off the porch. He didn't even think the two young people heard him as they continued engrossed in their conversation about cats. Mike chuckled.

"I've never seen this side of my nephew. I think he's completely infatuated with Brittany."

Erin smiled. "Brit's never taken an interest in a young man. Jason's completely swept her off her feet!"

She and Mike shared a laugh. He again recognized how comfortable he felt with her. Yes, she stirred his physical appetite, but he also experienced a simple, sincere closeness when they were together. The chemistry mingled with the friendship melded into a delightful companionship, and he relished both the feelings and the moments. He allowed his hand to brush hers. This time Erin took the initiative to interlock their fingers. He looked at her, and she smiled.

"Wouldn't it be something if my nephew and your daughter formed a relationship? Perhaps we'd see more of each other," Mike said.

Erin shrugged. "We don't have to depend on them to see each other."

He stopped walking and looked into her eyes.

"Are you saying you want to see each other after you leave the ranch?"

"I'm saying I'm open to the idea."

He squeezed her hand. "I'll take that. I'm open to the idea, too."

"Perhaps Thanksgiving?"

"Perhaps October?"

She smiled. "Perhaps. Let's just enjoy right now."

He nodded, and he tucked her hand into his elbow. "I'm doing that."

They continued to walk.

"What about your horse?" Mike asked.

"I'd like for you to train her if you're willing."

He smiled. "I'm willing. Would you like to visit Shadow? I think we should introduce her to Winston."

"I think you're right," Erin said. "And I think you may just see me back here in October."

Mike stopped walking again and looked at her. "I'd like that."

Erin smiled. "So would I."

His eyes bored into hers. "Erin, I'd…I want to…" He took a deep breath. "May I kiss you?"

Her smile widened. "You may."

Mike dipped his head and gently pressed his lips to hers. She tasted salty and sweet simultaneously. He kept himself in check and held her loosely. He felt her deepen the kiss and entwine an arm around his neck. Mike dropped Winston's leash and enfolded his arms more solidly around her waist. Erin's return embrace felt delicious and comforting at the same time. As their lips parted, each breathlessly clung to the other. After a moment, Mike said in a husky voice, "Well. That was certainly nice."

Erin gave him a brief, soft smile. He kissed her lips quickly and again tucked her hand into his elbow. He bent down and picked up Winston's leash. Looking at the small dog, Mike said, "Okay, buddy, let's go. I have my own canine pla I'd like you to meet. I think you'll like her."

# Chapter 20

**THE NEXT** morning, Erin and Brittany walked onto the cabin porch. A Toyota Highlander parked near the lodging across the gravel lot indicated the family expected by Maggie and Mike had arrived late last night.

"I vaguely remember hearing a vehicle pull in," Brittany commented as they took the steps down to the graveled area.

"I didn't hear a thing," Erin responded.

Brittany smiled. "I can understand why. You and Mike stayed up another hour after your walk."

Erin returned her daughter's smile. "You and Jason talked yourselves out during our stroll."

Brittany nodded. "We could have gone on longer, but since he had driven that distance and we'd all gone out to eat, he needed sleep, he said."

"You really like him, don't you?"

Brittany blushed. "I'm as amazed as you. I've never had so much in common with a guy before. And he's so gorgeous!" Erin laughed. "Well, he is!" her daughter said, a near pout in her voice.

"I'm not disagreeing with you. I've just never heard you talk like this. You're so much like your father and your aunt—so career-focused. I'm surprised, that's all. Happy for you, but surprised."

Brittany shrugged. "I don't know if it will go very far, we live such a distance apart."

"But you'd like it to go somewhere?"

Her daughter blushed again. "I'd like to try."

"Well, first make sure there's not a girl waiting for him in Washington, and if there's not, then simply ask him his thoughts. I witnessed the chemistry between you two, and if you both want to give a long-distance relationship a try for this next year, I say go for it!" She hugged Brittany's shoulder. "We both know life is too short to not try to capture love and happiness."

Brittany leaned onto her mother. "Thanks, Mom. You're right. I invited Jason over for dinner; I hope that's okay."

"You want me to scoot, I take it."

Brittany looked at her. "I hope you don't mind. Of course, I'm not sure where you'll go…"

"I've been invited horseback riding this evening. I wasn't sure…"

"Mike?" Erin nodded. "You should go. He seems like a caring man, and I can see how much he thinks of you."

"You can?"

"Mom, the man loves you. He tries to conceal it, but it's there. Do you love him?"

"I…I don't know."

"But you'd like to find out?"

"I would," Erin whispered.

"Like you said, life's too short. Take that horseback ride, enjoy yourself. After all, you're a horse owner now."

They came to the Kitty Castle. Erin kissed her daughter's cheek.

"Have a good morning, sweetie. I'll see you at lunch."

"Good luck with that grant. See you later, Mom."

Erin continued her walk to the administrative office. She stopped by the barn and greeted the paint. As she stroked the horse's nose, she whispered, "Well, girl, it seems you and I have a journey ahead of us. I hope you'll be nice to Mike and let him train you. I want to ride you one day. We have a connection, and I want us to enjoy life together."

The horse nickered and nuzzled her cheek.

Erin lay her head against the mare's cheek and stroked her neck.

"You're a special one, that's for sure."

"She thinks you are, too," came Mike's voice. Erin looked at him, standing near Cisco's stall. "I think you are, too."

Erin smiled. "So, about that horseback ride this evening. The answer is yes."

He grinned.

In the office a few hours later, Erin pulled back from the computer and shouted, "Done!"

Her excitement seemed contagious, as Kaitlyn and Maggie yelled, "Hooray!"

"Now," Erin said in a calmer tone, "we just have to wait about two months to find out the verdict."

"That will take us out of construction season," Maggie said, a frown forming on her face. "Even if we do get the grant."

"When will you hear on the tourism grant?"

"Maybe a week," Kaitlyn replied. "We had hoped to hear by now."

"When does the Chamber meet again?" Erin asked as she worried her lower lip.

"Tomorrow," Maggie replied.

Erin's eyes lit up, and she looked at Maggie. "Why don't you ask then? Tell them the situation and see if the tourism board will at least give you a yeah or nay. If it's yes, perhaps the lumber store will work with you to be paid later."

"Couldn't hurt," Kaitlyn said.

"How about you go with me?" Maggie said, looking at Erin. "You could speak as a visitor, how this place touched you and helped you adopt and become a volunteer?"

"Brittany and I are supposed to leave in two days. Tomorrow's packing day."

"Can your daughter handle that?"

"Oh, I'm sure if she got herself out here in less than a day, she can handle packing me up as well as preparing the cats. Yes, I'll go with you."

Maggie and Kaitlyn smiled at each other and then at Erin.

That evening, Mike and Erin rode horses into the high pasture. Shadow tagged beside Cisco, who carried two saddlebags. Their dinner was packed on one side, consisting of baked chicken, roasted zucchini, and cucumber salad. Mike also had slipped in a bottle of Pinot Grigio and utensils, along with stoneware dishes and glasses, all wrapped in cloth napkins. A blanket awaited in the other saddlebag for comfort while sitting on the ground.

The horse he provided Erin, a red roan mare, followed Cisco's trail from the lower pasture as the company wound around rocks and sagebrush. The hill rose above the sanctuary buildings to a large grove of Ponderosa pines supplemented by quaking aspen. Mike and his buckskin led the way toward the tree grove.

"It's lovely here," Erin commented.

Mike looked back and smiled. "One of my favorite places on the ranch. Oftentimes I find the Belgians back in the trees on warm days. They were here earlier."

"I hope they show up; I'd like to see them again before I leave," Erin said.

That soft reminder felt like a Chuck Norris kick to Mike's stomach. However, he masked the hurt as he replied, "We just might. They were in this area last time you saw them."

He stopped Cisco near an open meadow and commanded Shadow to 'stay.' He was impressed with the dog's intelligence and willingness to please. Mike dismounted, removed the saddlebags, and set them on the boulder. Again, he gave the 'stay' command. He then walked to Erin and her horse, and he helped her finish dismounting from the animal. As he held her, he gazed into her eyes.

"I wish this didn't have to be our last evening together."

She gave him a slight smile. "No one said it was. Maybe for now, but not forever."

He gave her a quick kiss on the lips and then smiled. "I'm glad about that." He stepped away from her. "There's a blanket in the left saddlebag. Why don't you spread it out while I tie up Belle and Cisco? I'll bring the food in a moment."

Erin nodded and walked toward the large rock where the saddlebags waited. She patted Shadow's head and then removed the woven blanket and spread it upon the ground. She looked around. A small creek danced over rocks nearby as it flowed from the higher elevations, zigzagging across the forest and lower hillside. The overlook offered a vantage point to gaze upon the meadow, the surrounding mountains, and the sanctuary buildings below. She sighed. Mike walked to her side and placed an arm around her waist.

"Nice, isn't it?"

"Oh, more than that—it's gorgeous! Thank you for bringing me here."

"Anytime." He grinned at her. "Dinner awaits, my lady."

Erin placed a hand on his cheek. "I can't believe you did all this for me. How come I am so blessed?"

Mike picked up her hand and kissed the top of her knuckle.

"Because I think you're incredibly special."

His mouth captured her lips in a passionate kiss and savored the way her body melded with his.

A few hours later, a fire crackled amid the ring of rocks Mike had gathered. As Erin sat next to him, gazing upon the meadow, warmth enveloped her. The horses stood nearby, munching on grass. Shadow lay to her right. The blaze took the chill from the late summer evening, but Mike's presence, with his arm draped across her shoulder, also warmed her physically and emotionally. The meal and wine filled her stomach as well as her heart and mind. Erin realized she hadn't felt this relaxed and comfortable since Daniel's diagnosis. Now, here she was, in a beautiful part of the world amid an animal rescue sanctuary, doing positive work and experiencing the love of a kind, caring man.

Mike's whisper near her ear disrupted her thoughts. "See that?"

She looked at him and then in the direction on which he focused his eyes. A herd of ten elk, cows and calves, captured her attention. Her eyes widened as she inhaled deeply.

"Oh, wow!" she whispered.

Shadow responded either to their voices or to the smell of the animals, for she suddenly sat up.

"Easy, girl," Mike said in a low, but firm tone. "Stay."

Erin captured the dog's leash, affixed to her red collar, in her hand.

"Thanks," Mike acknowledged, still speaking in a soft voice. "We're seeing females with their young. The males will start coming out, and they will be bugling soon."

"What does that mean?" Erin asked quietly.

"Usually in early September the bulls, male elk, come into what's known as the rut – the mating season. They make this incredible noise, called a bugle, that announces to other bulls it's time to fight for females. It's an amazing sound and an incredible experience to witness."

"I'd love to see that sometime."

Mike's gaze turned to her. "Whenever you want to come back in September, I'll bring you back up here, and we'll do just that."

She smiled and snuggled into his shoulder. After a quick pat to Shadow's head, Erin returned her gaze to the majestic wild creatures. A contented, soft sigh escaped, and she felt Mike's embrace tighten around her.

# Chapter 21

ERIN AND Maggie sat at an elongated table at the Cody County Chamber of Commerce meeting the next day. A group of twenty businesspeople and governmental officials occupied the other seats. A man about fifty pounded a gavel to conclude the discussion that had ensued and announced, "Okay, next order of business. This isn't on your agenda because it just came to my attention a few minutes prior to the meeting. The topic would generally be discussed at our next meeting, however, due to extenuating circumstances, I told Maggie I'd allow her to bring up the subject today."

He looked at the Compassion Ranch director. "Maggie, would you introduce your guest and explain to the members, many of which serve on the Tourism Board, why you want to talk about the grant at this time?"

Maggie rose and said, "Thank you, Chuck, I appreciate this opportunity." She glanced at those gathered around the table. "I'd like you all to meet Erin Christensen. She's a recent volunteer at Compassion Ranch, traveling through our area on her way back to her home in Florida. I've asked her to speak about her experience as she and her daughter leave tomorrow for their long drive home."

She looked at Erin and then sat down. Erin rose from her chair, walked behind it, and gave the gathering a smile.

"Thank you, everyone. I'm happy to be here." She took a deep breath and then exhaled. She smiled again and said, "I first heard about Compassion Ranch from my sister, who has a rescue in Montana, about ninety miles northwest of Yellowstone Park. She and I stopped in earlier this year after a trip to Denver for a conference. I was impressed with what I saw and learned during that brief visit, and I decided that on my way home to Florida, I'd spend a week or two volunteering. I love the mission of Compassion Ranch, and I've experienced first-hand the good work done there. From rescuing animals that would be euthanized if the sanctuary didn't exist to adopting out such animals, providing a home and a family for the animals and providing beloved companions to people. People like me and my daughter who lost a husband and father to cancer. People like the family now at the ranch who lost a beloved pet earlier this year and have fallen in love with one of the dogs that has been at the ranch for several months."

Erin paused and took a deep breath and then continued, "Maggie and her staff also educate school children and ranch visitors about the plight of research animals and the joy of pet adoption. It's a special place, a place of beauty, of connecting, of joy as well as sorrow, but most of all it's a place of healing, for both people and animals. I've experienced that first-hand as a widow and as a volunteer. The ranch needs a new building to continue their mission. Recently, a group of horses arrived and before that, several additional cats and dogs. The ranch brings visitors who bring dollars to this community through an extra stay, an extra meal or two, and likely additional shopping. I believe your tourism grant would be well-served helping Compassion Ranch. As a visitor, I'm certainly glad the sanctuary is here, and I'm sure other area visitors would concur."

She took another breath and then smiled. "Thank you for letting me speak."

Erin noticed people looking at each other as she sat down. The man who spoke earlier looked at her and asked, "Ms. Christiansen, during your time at the ranch, you stayed at the sanctuary, not in town, is that correct?"

"Yes, sir, that's right."

"And as a volunteer, I assume you weren't charged for your lodging."

Erin glanced at Maggie. "Yes, that's correct."

"So, you really didn't contribute to the community's coffers."

"Not so." Erin saw the man raise his eyebrows. "I brought groceries in town on two occasions. My daughter and I shopped for pet supplies and other items because we adopted two cats. We also went out to lunch, and twice I've been to dinner in the community. Before I leave town today, I'll be shopping for gifts for family and friends. So, Mr. Wilson, I have contributed to your community's economy in several different ways even though I stayed at the ranch."

The man nodded. "Thank you. I appreciate your insights."

Maggie stood. "If I may, I'd like to add to what Erin had to say." She looked at Chuck Wilson, and he nodded.

"At Compassion Ranch in the past week, we've brought in twelve dogs, ten cats, and four horses, as Erin said," Maggie explained. "Two of our sheep have given birth, one having a difficult first several hours. We need to expand, especially our barn and our intake areas. We adopted two cats to Erin and her daughter, and two dogs to two different families. We've had interest in a few of the horses we recently received. Animals are finding homes, but more will be coming in yet this fall. We applied for a tourism grant, and we'd like to apply that money, if we are indeed on the receiving end, for construction. As you all know, that window of opportunity around here will close soon, and with such a small staff, we need each day of good weather we can get. I want to ask if you would tell me if our sanctuary is on the list to be granted funds? If we are, I can approach Brad Singer for credit on the lumber and hardware until the grant money is dispensed. Thank you for letting me speak."

She sat down. Wilson looked around the room. "Ladies and gentlemen, any questions for our guest or for Maggie?"

A woman two seats to Maggie's left spoke up. "Maggie, how long has Compassion Ranch been here now?"

"We're approaching eighteen years."

"How many tourism grants have you been given during that time?"

"Only one, during our third year when we built the cabins for guests."

"How many times have you applied?"

With sadness in her voice, Maggie said, "Five times."

The woman nodded. "Thank you." She looked around the room. "That's one reason I voted to give funds this year to Compassion Ranch. I know many people in the area, in this room in fact, who see the sanctuary as a detriment because it's viewed as not 'cowboy enough.' So what if they don't raise beef cattle or sheep? So what if they don't allow hunting on the property? That's not what this place is about. I for one believe there's room for different types of property—dude ranches for guests as well as working ranches to supply food, and hunting ranches for out-of-state game and fish seekers. The point is each one contributes to our local and state economy. Each attracts a different type of visitor. One is not better than the other, but each one is needed for clientele and visitors who come to our region. All fill a special spot in our community."

A white-haired man next to her nodded. "I concur with Carla. I've been on the fence about Compassion Ranch, wondering what they did besides rescue animals, but upon hearing from Ms. Christiansen, I'm no longer uncertain. Since I was the last holdout, Chuck, you can tell Maggie what was decided last week because I'm in agreement."

Chuck Wilson, moderator of the Chamber meeting, nodded. He looked toward Maggie and Erin, sitting at the opposite end of the table from him, and said, "Maggie, it's my pleasure to tell you the Tourism Board will grant you a check next month in the amount of $7,500 dollars. I know that's not enough to build a large barn, but hopefully enough to get things started, or maybe apply the funds toward another need."

Maggie stood, a large smile on her face. "Thank you, thank you all. With that grant and one given by Erin's family foundation, we'll have enough to construct the building we need."

Erin felt everyone's eyes on her. Mr. Wilson asked, "Ms. Christiansen—you are contributing to the construction fund?"

She nodded and stood next to Maggie. "My late husband set up a foundation before his passing. My children and I agreed to use part of that money to help Compassion Ranch, and since this barn is vital, we planned to give toward that project. I'm honored we can partner on this project."

"Well, thank you for investing in our community through Compassion Ranch," Wilson stated. "We hope you will return sometime."

Erin smiled. "My pleasure. And I will."

The man dropped the gavel and announced, "All right then. Since this was the last item on our agenda, I call for the dismissal of the Tourism Board and the Cody County Chamber of Commerce meeting. Thank you all for being here."

Maggie turned to Erin and hugged her. "Thank you," she whispered, "thank you so much."

As Erin and Maggie stepped out of a store and onto the downtown boardwalk, Erin's large smile shone brightly.

"I hope Mr. Wilson sees me with all these packages before we leave town," she said.

Maggie laughed. "We could swing by his office and just say 'thanks' again."

"Perhaps we should. What type of business is he in?"

"He runs a restaurant."

"Let's stop by for a cup of tea and a snack of some kind."

"They do serve pie there."

"Let's do that!" Erin said with a grin.

The two women shared a laugh and then proceeded down the street, Maggie leading the way. Within a block, she turned toward a glass door and opened it. Erin followed her inside. A young blonde waitress seated them, and after Maggie ordered a cup of coffee and Erin requested a cup of black tea, the women reviewed the pie list. When the server returned with their beverages, Maggie said, "I believe I'll have a slice of the pecan pie."

"Sounds good," the waitress said. "And for you, ma'am?"

"I'll try the lemon meringue," Erin said.

The waitress smiled. "Our specialty."

"Is Chuck here?" Maggie inquired, looking at their server.

"Yes. Do you want me to ask him to stop by your table?"

Maggie smiled. "If you would please. We attended the Chamber meeting and just wanted to thank him again for his help."

The girl nodded and left.

Erin smiled. "You're devilish, Maggie."

"Hey, you agreed to this."

Erin's smile remained on her face. "We're both devilish."

"That's one reason we make a good team. Erin, I want to ask you…"

Maggie's statement was cut off by Chuck Wilson walking to and standing beside their table.

"Ladies. Stopping in for some pie, I understand," he commented.

"I didn't want Erin to leave without experiencing your homemade pies, Chuck," Maggie said with a smile.

He looked at Erin. "I hope you'll stay longer next time, Ms. Christiansen. Our Italian dinners are quite famous around here."

"That is true," Maggie affirmed, "especially the lasagna and the stuffed pasta shells."

Erin smiled. "Next time for sure. Maggie and I have been shopping this afternoon, Mr. Wilson. I'm a person of my word. I'm contributing to the local economy." She nodded to the bags under the table. "My friends and family members will have a taste of Cody from my time in the area."

Chuck bowed. "Our community thanks you."

In a more serious tone, he said as he looked at her, "Thank you for helping Compassion Ranch as a volunteer and supporter and thank you for coming to our humble town. I do hope next time you'll come and enjoy a meal here. I'm intrigued by your family foundation and what types of projects you support. The economy here is up and down, as you might understand. We could use more people who enjoy our area spending time here and helping us market."

"I'll keep that all in mind, Mr. Wilson. I appreciate the opportunity to speak today."

He nodded as the waitress returned with their snack. "Ladies. Enjoy your pies. They're on me."

He walked away, and after their server set the desserts in front of them, she, too, departed. Erin and Maggie took a small bite of their respective pies. Erin savored the tanginess of the lemon and the flavorful graham cracker crust.

"Delicious!" she said.

Maggie nodded. "Chuck and his sous chef

and other staff are great cooks and bakers. He's made a good life with this restaurant. Speaking of which, there's something I want to discuss with you, Erin, something I hope will interest you."

"I'm all ears."

"I'd like you to come on staff with us at Compassion Ranch."

Erin stared at the woman seated across from her. "What?!"

"You're talented, organized, detailed and diligent. I need someone like you."

"Maggie, I'm flattered, but I'm not looking for a job."

"I know, but as our operations grow, as they are doing, Kaitlyn isn't able to keep up."

"Kaitlyn. Oh, Maggie, I can't replace her! She told me the other day that's been her greatest fear. She has a wedding coming up. "

"She told you that? Oh, goodness, no! I don't mean you'd replace her. She's valuable to me. It's just that she's stretched so thin, and I need her to focus on what she does best, which is bookkeeping, membership, and tour arrangements, as well as my schedule and correspondence. I need you, Erin, for grant writing and marketing."

"Grant writing? That's part of Kaitlyn's job."

Maggie nodded. "Yes, but it's all too much. I want to take some things off her plate so she can focus on those, as I said, she does best. Like all our staff, you'll be a great asset to the organization."

"Maggie, I'm flattered, truly, but my home is in Florida."

The sanctuary director nodded again. "Of course. I'm talking about a virtual job with visits back at times. With your kids in college and ready to start their lives as career-minded adults and your sister living nearby, I thought my offer might be an intriguing idea for you. Work from home and come back here periodically."

Erin pondered a few moments while eating more of her pie.

"It is intriguing," she responded a bit later. "Are you sure though that the non-profit can afford to do this?"

Maggie smiled. "Well, that depends on how much you'd charge. I can tell you the Board is all for it; I've already talked with them. I'm not taking a salary increase this year and neither is Mike. We might not take an increase the year after either I want to distribute that between you and Kaitlyn. As you said, she's getting married next year, and I want her to be happy in her job and be able to have the wedding she wants."

Maggie sighed and glanced out the

restaurant's bay window nearby. "I had no idea Kate had such a concern about her job. I guess I have some speaking to do with that girl."

"And, I have some thinking to do," Erin said.

Maggie looked at her and smiled.

Erin and Brittany sat in the living room, Winston curled on Erin's lap as she sat in the recliner and Brittany engaged in play with her cats on the couch.

"So, what do you think?" Erin asked her daughter after telling her of her conversation with Maggie earlier.

"I think the job sounds fabulous! You should take it."

"You really think so?"

Brittany paused in her attention to the cats. "Mom, you love this place and you love being with Aunt Rhiann. You can do both when you come out here. And you don't have to always be here, you can work from the house in Florida, so you don't have to spend winters here. You have opportunity to use your skills for a great cause. I say take it!"

Erin smiled. "Well, it's only part-time and like you said, I can research and write from home, email and Skype with Maggie…"

"Speaking of Skype, Jason and I are going to be doing that."

"You are?"

Brittany smiled and nodded and returned to playing with the cats. "We exchanged emails and social media information."

"I thought you quit a lot of that stuff except for that Snapchat thing."

Her daughter smiled and then shrugged. "I still Instant Message, and a lot of Jason's research is on Facebook and LinkedIn. I'll be connecting with him in those ways, too."

"Sounds like the two of you want to stay in touch." She smiled. "I'm happy for you, Brit."

A blush came over Brittany's face. "We exchanged cell numbers too."

"Sounds like you parted on a hopeful note. I'm glad for you, sweetheart. Just take it slow."

"What about you and Mike?"

"He and I have an understanding."

"I like him, Mom."

"Jason?"

"Well, yes, but Mike—I like him, and I think he's good for you."

Erin smiled. "Well, I have asked him to train my horse, and if I do take this job, I'll likely be seeing him from time to time."

Brittany gazed at her mother. "Take the job."

Erin looked at her daughter and a small smile crossed her face. "Thank you for the support, honey. I'm considering it."

# Chapter 22

**AT SEVEN** o'clock the next morning, Erin and Brittany loaded the car with Erin's clothing-filled suitcases and the two bags which Brittany had brought on the plane. They also packed the gifts Erin purchased the day previous, putting them into small boxes which Maggie had given them last night. At that time, Erin had provided her answer regarding the job; however, she asked Maggie to not reveal it to the rest of the staff.

"I'll do that before Brit and I leave."

Now, as Erin tidied up the bathroom, making sure the items she and Brittany owned were cleared out, she heard her daughter shout, "Mom! We have company!"

A tap sounded from the back porch. Erin walked out of the bathroom as Brittany opened the cabin door and said, "Hey, there, Mike. Come on in. Oh! Who's this?"

Erin heard Mike respond, "This is Gary Anderson. He has a summer job with the Forest Service but volunteers with us on occasion. I asked him to help me with the livestock this morning and then he's going to help at the Dog Palace later. I thought since he's here early, maybe we could help you ladies get things packed up."

"That's nice of you both," Brittany replied. "Come on in. We still have coffee, and I'm sure Mom would appreciate you helping us finish it."

"I wouldn't mind a cup," Erin heard an unfamiliar baritone voice say.

She stepped into view and looked at the two men. Mike, dressed in gently-worn blue jeans and a light blue cotton short-sleeved shirt, looked at her and smiled. The man standing near Mike gave her a quick smile and brief nod. His faded jeans and wrinkled short-sleeved red shirt indicated his readiness to work.

"Good morning," Erin welcomed the two men as she smiled at them.

"Good morning to you," Mike said. "Erin and Brittany Christiansen, this is Gary Anderson."

Erin shook hands with the twenty-something Forest Service worker/Compassion Ranch volunteer. Brittany nodded her head at him as she poured two cups of coffee.

"Nice to meet you, Gary," Erin stated.

"Same here, ma'am. Mike says you're heading out today?"

She nodded. "I've been here close to three weeks, and my daughter needs to get back home to start her last semester of college."

Gary looked at Brittany. "I'm finishing my degree in the spring. What are you studying?"

"Marine biology. I'm hoping to work with dolphins or sea turtles after school."

Gary smiled. "Wildlife biology's my major. I've been on the six-year-plan because of some family stuff. My specialty is fisheries."

"Sounds cool. What are you working on with the Forest Service?" Brittany asked.

"Stream studies and brook trout." He accepted the cup of coffee Brittany offered. "Thanks. I spend three to four days a week in the Absaroka and Beartooth ranges and a day or so in the office writing up my findings."

"Oh, it's beautiful up there!"

Erin noticed Gary look at Brittany in surprise. "You've been up to the high country?"

She nodded. "A few times. We have family in Montana." Brittany then looked at Erin. "Mom, would you like a cup? Got just enough for one more."

"How about putting it in my to-go mug? We should be hitting the road soon."

"Everything ready to go?" Mike asked as

Brittany handed him a cup of steaming liquid from the coffee pot. "Thanks, Brittany."

She nodded at him and began rinsing out the glass carafe.

"Just finishing," Erin responded. "I was about to head down to the office, taking Winston's last sanctuary walk before we go."

"You two go," Brittany said. "I still have to get Ricky and Rocket's travel bags and carriers."

"I can take your stuff to the car," Gary offered as he looked from one woman to the other.

"That would be nice, thank you," Erin said. She looked at her daughter. "Is that okay with you?"

The young woman shrugged. "I have no problem with it."

"Who are Ricky and Rocket?" Gary asked.

Brittany grinned. "My newly adopted cats."

"Cool! Can I meet them?"

Brittany scooped her cell phone off the kitchen counter. "I've got pictures I can show you first. Then we can get them from their lounging spot in the other room."

Erin gathered Winston's leash and snapped it to his collar. "My packed bags are on the couch,

Erin." She dug the car keys out of the pocket of her khakis. "Here are the car keys."

Brittany accepted her mother's offering and then began showing Gary photos of her new feline companions. Erin smiled at Mike, who returned her expression. She beckoned Winston to her, and the little dog obeyed.

"We'll be back in a short while," she commented to Brittany and Gary. Her daughter waved her off.

Erin, Winston, and Mike walked onto the porch. She stopped at the bottom of the steps and surveyed the landscape.

"It's so beautiful here," Erin breathed. "I will miss this."

"Erin, I…" Mike started.

She looked at him. "Let's walk and talk."

She and Winston led the way as they strolled along the gravel parking area. Erin noticed the family staying at the cabin across the way must still be at the sanctuary for their Highlander was parked in the lot.

"I see the Browns are still here," Erin commented. "Has Leslie been able to use them during their stay?"

Mike nodded. "They're very enthusiastic and

have worked well with the dogs and cats. Livestock wasn't their thing."

He grinned, and she returned his smile. "It wasn't mine until recently."

"Speaking of, are you going to name your horse before you leave or shall I just keep referring to her as 'hey, you' and 'Erin's horse?'"

Her smile grew larger. "She has a name."

"Really? What is it?"

"You'll find out when we get there."

They walked in silence for a few moments. Mike stretched out his hand, and after looking into his eyes for a few seconds, Erin enfolded her free hand into his. They continued their stroll to the barn.

"Erin, I need to tell you a few things before you leave." Mike's deep voice conveyed a sad, serious tone. "I'm in love with you, and I know you've known that for a bit. I also know you need more time to figure out your future without Daniel. I'm here, and I'll be waiting. If you decide pursuing a relationship outside of friendship with me is not something you want to do, I'll understand. I won't stop loving you because I haven't for over thirty years. But I don't want you leaving and feeling pressured. I'm content with my life here, and I'm accepting whatever decision you make about us in the future. I will miss you, but at a minimum, I'm thankful for our reconnection and friendship."

"I am, too, Mike." She stopped beside the pasture fence. She gazed at the surrounding landscape "Being here, spending time with you, it's all been wonderful. I will likely be back, maybe sooner than originally expected." She turned and looked at him. With a smile, she continued, "Maggie offered me a part-time job yesterday." She paused, and her smile widened. "I said 'yes.'"

His eyes grew large. "You did?!"

She nodded. "Brittany and I talked about it, and she was very encouraging."

He grinned. "I knew I liked that girl!"

Erin chuckled. "I'll be working from home a lot, from Florida, especially during the winter. I'll help Maggie with grants and fundraising events, so I'll return off and on during the rest of the year. I'll be able to visit my sister as well. Starting next month." She grinned. "So, hearing those elk bugle— is that still a date?"

Mike laughed. "Of course!" His hands enveloped her forearms. His face took on a solemn expression and with a hoarse whisper, he said, "I'm happy for you, Erin. You'll be good at that work, and you'll be a great right-hand person for Maggie."

"I'm not taking Kaitlyn's job. I'll be a virtual helper with some aspects of the sanctuary's marketing, including grant writing. I'll make the occasional trip back…just likely not in winter."

She said her last statement with a smile. Mike grinned and replied, "I can understand that. It's really wonderful that you're joining the staff—you'll be great! We'll be able to see each other more often than I thought."

"And we can see what the future might hold for us."

"So, you're…you're willing to give it a try?" Mike asked, searching her face.

She nodded and smiled. "I am. As I said before, I'm very blessed to be loved by two fine men."

Mike's lips captured hers with a crushing, passionate kiss. The power and fire took her breath away. Dropping Winston's leash, she wrapped her arms around Mike's neck and drew his body closer. As their lips tasted each other in a hungry manner, Erin's heart hammered. Simultaneously, she felt Mike's heart thunder in his chest as his arms tightened around her waist. She relished the synchronicity of their hearts, and she lavished the feel of his brawny strength. Coolness sapped her when he broke from the embrace.

"You take my breath away," he said, a husky flavor to his voice.

"There's more where that came from," she replied, her own voice sultry.

Mike growled, and his lips captured hers again. She enjoyed the passionate fire between them. After he pulled his mouth from hers, Mike murmured as he still held her, "These kisses are seared upon my lips and heart, giving me added memories until I see you again."

Erin gave a small laugh and watched a grin come to Mike's face. "Well, it won't be long. After the kids are settled back into college, I'll be meeting Rhiann and Levi here—they're interested in the horses as pasture companions for their herd. So, you have some work ahead of you, mister!"

Mike gave a hearty laugh. "Between you and Maggie, I don't know if I'll have any fall fishing time!" He put his arm across her shoulder and together they turned to look at the horses. "It's all worth it, though."

He leaned over and kissed her check as the paint trotted up to them.

"I wanted to make sure you had the right incentive to take good care of Scout for me," Erin said in a teasing tone.

She extended her hand toward the mare.

"Scout, eh? Great name."

"I thought so. She scouted me out and

provided guidance…as did you."

Mike hugged her to his side as Erin stroked her horse's face.

"I think we're guiding each other," Mike whispered. "Finding one another here at Compassion Ranch, we've discovered many beautiful things—the animals, the mission of the sanctuary, new friends…" He turned her toward him. "Love."

Erin smiled, and she gazed at Mike. Their lips met in a tender kiss.

# Epilogue

**PALM TREES** swayed in the breeze. Mike's wavy brown and silver hair parroted the movement as he stood on the sandy beach. Ocean waves crashed against the pier to his right as the tide lapped his ankles. He inhaled the salty fragrance while his lips tasted the sparkling crystals sprinkled by the sea. The late afternoon sun kissed the horizon, threatening to dip into the ocean. The crisp orange and bright crimson colors of the sky mesmerized him. He'd come to relish Florida sunsets during the past two weeks.

As he stared at the sky and the waves, he felt a light caress upon his shoulder. He turned his head and caught the beautiful face and delicious smile of his love. Mike dipped his head and placed a light kiss upon Erin's lips.

"Enjoying another evening sunset, I see," she whispered.

Mike returned his gaze to the ocean. "I must admit, I like Florida in January."

"Really? I hadn't noticed," came Erin's light, teasing voice.

He glanced at her and grinned. He then raised

his hand and brushed some strands of her silky dark hair from her face.

"Sunsets are great, 80-degree weather is awesome, but you know what the best part of January in Florida is?"

Her smile deepened. "What?"

"You."

His husky whisper brought a bat of Erin's dark eyelashes. As she leaned into him, shoeless toes touched his feet. His heart leaped and his breath quickened from that simple touch, and the heat of her lips against his seared his mouth. Mike drew Erin closer, his hands locking around her waist. Her arms encircled his neck. As she trailed light kisses along his cheek, her voice whispered like silk upon his ear.

"I told you winter in Florida is grand."

# From the Author:

Thank you for reading Erin and Mike's story about *Finding Love at Compassion Ranch.* This is Book #2 in my series "Pet Rescue Romance." Book #1, *Rescue Road*, is the story of Erin's sister, Rhiann, who moves to Montana after the death of their grandmother, having purchased land for back taxes, land that was settled more than 100 years previous by their grandmother's father. There she meets Levi Butler, the local EMS supervisor, who believes the land is his, inherited from his mentor and friend, George. Someone else wants to lay claim to the ranch, a wily investor named Dallas Patterson. Who will the ranch ultimately go to, and can Rhiann and Levi set aside their differences and travel the rescue road together? The book is available in print and e-book format from Amazon (https://amzn.to/2MCklLl); at Barnes & Noble (http://bit.ly/2BAvqWZ), and on Kobo (http://bit.ly/2PaUOus).

Learn more about my books, including my children's works and Christian dog-lovers devotions on my Amazon page: https://amzn.to/37WMk0V

### *Gayle M. Irwin*

# ABOUT THE AUTHOR

**Gayle M. Irwin** is an award-winning author and freelance writer who lives in Wyoming. She is a contributor to seven *Chicken Soup for the Soul* books and the author of inspirational pet books for children and adults. She weaves important life lessons within her stories, including courage, kindness, perseverance, nature appreciation, and the importance of pet rescue and adoption. She volunteers for rescue organizations and donates a percentage of book sales to such groups. Her own pets are rescues that she and her husband adopted. Her first romance novel, *Rescue Road*, about a freelance writer turned animal rescue advocate who falls in love with a local EMS supervisor, was published in November 2019; it is the first story in her Pet Rescue Romance series. *Finding Love at Compassion Ranch* is the second book in the series. Book 3 is planned for release Summer 2021, while the first book in her Christian, inspirational pet rescue romance, *Rescuing Sarah*, is planned for release in November 2020. Learn more about Gayle and her writing at www.gaylemirwinauthor.com.

# Recipes from Finding Love at Compassion Ranch

In the story, Mike packs an evening meal to share with Erin during a horseback ride the last night she's at Compassion Ranch. Below are recipes for a baked chicken dish, roasted zucchini, and cucumber salad as mentioned in the story:

## Baked Chicken with Herbs

Ingredients:
2 Chicken Breasts
Olive oil
Herbs/Spices, such as Italian seasoning; paprika; seasoning salt; pepper; rosemary; oregano; lemon juice; or Cajun.

Instructions:
Preheat the oven to 400 degrees F. Toss the chicken breasts with olive oil, herbs/spices. Lightly grease a baking dish or pan so the chicken breasts don't stick. Bake breasts for 22-26 minutes or until they reach 165°F. Let meat rest before slicing and serving.

Recipe from SpendWithPennies.com:
https://www.spendwithpennies.com/oven-baked-chicken-breasts/

## Roasted Zucchini Spears

Ingredients:
Zucchini squash
Olive oil
Salt & Pepper

## Recipes, continued:
## Roasted Zucchini Spears

Herbs/Spices, such as Italian seasoning; rosemary; or tarragon
Parmesan cheese
Lemon juice (optional)

Instructions:
Trim off the ends of zucchini, cut into halves, and then slice lengthwise into quarters (the "spear" approach). Hint: larger pieces of zucchini are less prone to overcooking (and thus becoming soggy). Drizzle zucchini with olive oil, salt, and pepper. Add any other spices you like, such as Italian seasoning and/or rosemary. Add some Parmesan cheese. Toss to coat the zucchini evenly.

Elevate the zucchini by placing spears on a baking rack and then setting that rack on top of a regular baking sheet. This allows air to circulate on all sides and helps water evaporate so the zucchini is caramelized, not soggy. Roast at 400 degrees F for 12 to 15 minutes or until tender.

Afterward, you may want to place the zucchini under the broiler so that the Parmesan becomes nice and crisp. For an additional pop, squeeze some fresh lemon juice over the top and sprinkle the zucchini with more fresh herbs

Recipe from WellPlated.com:
https://www.wellplated.com/roasted-zucchini/

## Recipes, continued:

## <u>Cool, Creamy Dilled Cucumber Salad</u>
<u>Ingredients:</u>
½ cup reduced-fat sour cream   ¾ tsp. garlic powder
2 Tbsps. cider vinegar (or white wine vinegar)
1 tsp. sugar               ¾ tsp dill weed
½ tsp salt                 3 medium cucumbers, sliced
½ cup sliced onion

<u>Instructions:</u>
Clean, slice, wash, and dry cucumbers.
In a bowl, combine sour cream, vinegar, sugar, garlic powder, dill, and salt. Add cucumbers and onion; toss to coat. Cover and refrigerate for at least 1 hour. Serve with slotted spoon.

Light & Tasty, 2002
Similar recipe found here:
https://www.tasteofhome.com/recipes/creamy-dilled-cucumber-salad/

# Upcoming Releases:

Book 3 in the Pet Rescue Romance series, *Paws-itively Love*, is set for release Summer 2021. Read the first chapter below:

# Chapter 1:

Brittany Christiansen stood at the main corral, phone in hand. For the tenth time that morning, she stared at the text, debating whether to delete the message. It would be the last communication she would have from Jason, a break-up message. *Do I really want to save this anymore? He's said we're over.* Her finger hovered over the trashcan symbol as she read his message once more.

"I'm really sorry to do this, Brit, but I'm going to be in the field all summer. We've struggled to maintain a long-distance relationship even with Facebook, Instagram, Facetime, text, and phone; how can we continue with very little communication the next three months? I think it's best if we went our separate ways. Neither of us know where we'll be come fall."

When she didn't respond, he'd sent one more quick text: "I've enjoyed getting to know you and seeing you a few more times since last August. I hope you'll eventually forgive me. I do like you, Brit, and I wish you well. Goodbye."

"Goodbye, Jason," she whispered, as she texted him a handwave emoji. She then deleted Jason's texts.

Brittany felt a hand on her shoulder. She turned her head slightly. Her Aunt Rhiann's face held a sober look.

"You okay, Brit?"

The twenty-five-year-old auburn-haired woman forced a smile. "I will be."

"Of course you will. I'm just sorry your first relationship ended with a text. That's pretty cold-hearted."

Brittany shrugged. "I'm sure I'm not the only one it's happened to." She sighed and turned her gaze back to the corral. Three horses munched on hay in the trough at the opposite end of the enclosure. "I should never have gotten my hopes up. We just clicked so strongly last summer when we met at Compassion Ranch. Things seemed great over spring break when he came here."

Her aunt squeezed her shoulder. "I know. I liked the guy, and I know your mom did, too. Of course, being married to Jason's uncle, she accepted Jason as family."

"I'm going to hold off telling mom – I don't want her relationship with Mike to be affected by this." Again, Brittany sighed. She plastered a smile on her face as she glanced at her aunt again. "I'm so happy you and Uncle Levi adopted these horses from Compassion Ranch this spring. They are beauties!"

She returned her gaze to the three horses: one red appaloosa, one bay with a black mane and tail, and one palomino.

"Levi has been working with them diligently, as we remember a certain young lady had her eyes on the appy," Rhiann said.

Brittany chuckled. "I'm grateful to Uncle Levi. I do hope I'll be able to ride her before the end of the summer."

"Oh, we're pretty sure you will be able to," Rhiann responded.

The sound of a motor and tires traveling the gravel drive caused both women to turn. A red Chevy pickup stopped near the house.

"I wonder who that is?" Brittany stated.

"One of our new helpers," her aunt responded.

Rhiann walked toward the truck, and Brittany followed.

A dark-haired man exited the driver's side of the pickup. As Brittany drew closer, she realized he looked familiar. She watched her aunt shake the man's hand.

"Good to see you again, Gary," Rhiann said. "We so appreciate your help with the pastures."

Brittany stopped next to her aunt and stared at the man. *He looks familiar,* she thought. *Did Aunt Rhiann just call him Gary?*

Gary Anderson smiled as he shook Rhiann's hand. "Good to be here. I'm happy to help."

He looked at the young woman next to the ranch owner. He noticed she stared at him, and he did a double-take.

"I know you," they said simultaneously.

Gary chuckled. "Brittany, right?" She nodded. "I'm Gary Patterson. I met you last summer at Compassion Ranch, the day you and your mom left."

Brittany laughed. "Wow, yeah! What are you doing here?"

"I'm helping Levi extend a pasture. What about you? Volunteering here at Martha's Pet Rescue Sanctuary for the summer?"

Brittany laughed and shook her head. "No, not exactly—I'm working here for the summer. Rhiann is my aunt and Levi is my uncle."

Gary stared at the lovely young woman for a moment and then looked at Rhiann, who was smiling.

"That's true. Brittany's mom is my sister. How amazing you two are here."

*Amazing indeed,* Gary thought, as he smiled at Brittany again.

"Well, looks like we might see a lot of each other this summer," he said aloud.

I am also planning to release a Christmas-themed novella in December 2020 – stay tuned!

FINDING LOVE AT COMPASSION RANCH

Made in the USA
Middletown, DE
01 August 2020